GW00708271

CROSS OF ROPE

Yale Braden had thought he would sell his ranch and move out to California. Rincon, New Mexico hadn't offered the peace he wanted so badly. He was sick of smelling burned powder and counting the dead, although he himself never carried a gun. Then Duel Ashfork returned to Rincon. He had escaped from a Mexican prison and had rustled two thousand head of cattle on his way north. He needed land—and Braden's was the perfect spread.

CROSS OF ROPE

Dudley Dean

First published by Berkley Books

This hardback edition 1996
by Chivers Press
by arrangement with
the Golden West Literary Agency

ISBN 0 7451 4681 3

British Library Cataloguing in Publication Data available

Printed and bound in Great Britain by
Redwood Books, Trowbridge, Wiltshire

CROSS OF ROPE

CHAPTER ONE

Duel Ashfork's come home!
My God!
Oil up your guns, boys!

This was the general reaction of the small cow outfits north and east of Rincon on this spring day at close of roundup, 1873.

Yale Braden of 88 received the news from Jeremiah Peters, who spurred a scrubby bay horse across Victoria Creek that early morning. Old man Peters, patriarch of the hill clan that ran cows deep in the Mogollons, was paying his first visit to 88 in the two years Yale had owned the place. Yale invited the old man to step down, but Peters violently shook his gray head.

"Just want to know how you stand, Braden." Peters' tight, mean little face poked out from a fuzz of white beard. "Duel's home with two thousand head of Mex cows. He'll need more range. First *yours*. Then *ours*."

"His brother once made me a proposition. If I ever wanted to sell, I was to give him first chance. Mark sent word this morning he wants to see me—"

"Before you sell to an Ashfork, you better think long and hard."

"I think that's my business, Peters."

Shaking his fist, Peters cried, "The hell with you, then," and sent his horse plunging up through the aspens, spurring it hard all the way to the ridge and out of sight.

Yale Braden's foreman, Bill Striker, had heard the exchange. Striker was a Texan, in his forties, with a face lined from weather and the tough years that had followed the war.

"What you aim to do, Yale?" Striker asked narrowly.

Yale, staring at the rise of the Mogollons against the New Mexican sky, considered his reply. Within the hour a Rafter A rider had arrived with a message. Mark Ashfork wanted to see him at the Gadsen House in Rincon this morning. Yale had been about to saddle up when Jeremiah Peters appeared to demand Yale state his position in the trouble that was

5

sure to shape up with the return of Mark Ashfork's younger brother.

Striker, with the lank build of the horseman, was standing hipshot, rolling a cigarette, awaiting Yale's reply.

Finally it came, carefully thought out. Yale standing tall, shoulders back as if he might be reviewing troops.

"Bill, I've been thinking that out in California a man could live a decent life without these pressures—"

"If you figure to go to town and dicker with Mark," Striker said coldly, "you better wear a gun."

"I'm quite capable of handling the situation in my own way." Yale smiled at his foreman's tight brown face. Striker did not return the smile. He stared at Yale as if seeing him for the first time. Yale Braden was rangy in build, with features not classic by any means but of sufficient strength to have caused a flurry among mothers with daughters of marriageable age in Rincon—despite the fact that he was Missouri Nawth.

"With Duel back home," Striker said evenly, "things won't be the same. Either tie on a gun or let me and the boys go with you."

"My business is with Mark, not his brother."

With a grunt, Striker turned down the path toward the bunkhouse.

Cutting for town on a roan, Yale crossed the south pasture of 88 to take a look at the white-stockinged black he was breaking to saddle. He intended it as a birthday present for Thela Wheatley. The black ran, head up, frisky as a colt in the morning sun. Yale watched it a few minutes, finding pleasure. He would take the horse with them to California. Now that he had made up his mind to pull out, he felt better.

In Rincon, eight miles over a mountain road, Yale left his roan at the livery. As was his habit since being given back his life, he savored the small sights and sounds; the lazy awkward movement of a furred tarantula across a rutted alley, the sound of the wind cutting into the aspens behind Quincy's Saloon. He enjoyed feeling the slatted walk under his boots. Even the spring New Mexican heat was not discomforting. For a dead man would not be aware of these sensations. He sucked the warm air into his lungs as he made the climb along Mesilla Street. It was five months since the ambusher's bullet had downed him in the Mogollons.

In the next block the Gadsen House put a long shadow across the dun-colored street. Yale Braden bent his tallness against the slanted walk. His hair ends bleached from the sun, the brown face a little grim, as if life had touched him brutally. Yet at times there was humor in his light gray eyes, a generous curling of his wide mouth.

Yale paused a moment in front of Quincy's Saloon to get his breath after the climb. It was comforting to note that his legs no longer trembled, so his recovery was complete.

As he stood there a man pushed wide shoulders through the swinging doors of Quincy's to regard him thinly.

"You're Yale Braden," the man said.

Although he had never seen the man, Yale knew it was Duel Ashfork. In his mid-twenties, younger than Yale by five years. Darkly handsome, with curving black mustache and insolent yellow eyes. Duel's gunbelt still had a shine of newness, and the walnut grips of his revolver were not yet darkened from handling. A new outfit, Yale thought, probably to replace the one confiscated by the Mexican authorities at *Ciudad Chihuahua*.

Duel said, "I hear you're our new neighbor."

"Two years hardly makes me new. I came here a few months after you—went away."

"Don't be afraid to say it," Duel said darkly. "I been in a Mex prison."

"And you escaped."

"Me and some other boys who didn't like it there much. And I come home with two thousand head of Mex cows. A thousand head for each year they had me locked up."

"Fair enough payment, I'd say."

Some men were looking on across the street, but Duel ignored them. He wore a sweated hat, the chin strap against the front of a wool shirt. His pants were striped, the boots freshly oiled.

"My brother could've ransomed me outa that prison. But he never bothered to send the goddam money."

"Perhaps it wasn't as easy to buy you out of prison as you thought."

Duel Ashfork showed white teeth in a sudden burst of laughter. "I figured you'd take Mark's part. I just wanted to be sure. I hear he saved your life."

"He did. Five months ago."

Duel had been leaning a hard shoulder against the saloon wall. He straightened up. "I need more grass for the cows I brought. And I don't like to neighbor with anybody named Braden."

"If you'll excuse me—"

7

Yale had started up the walk, but Duel blocked him. "I hear you're one of the Bradens from outa Sedalia."

"The Missouri trouble was some years back," Yale said stiffly. "Why don't you forget it?"

"A Texian will never forget it!" Duel made a cutting motion with a dark hand. "Four thousand dollars is too much for your Eighty-Eight brand, but I'll offer it. To get shut of you."

"You're much too generous. Now stand aside. I'm on my way to see Mark."

"You might be too late." Duel's yellow eyes were amused. "My brother's feeling poorly."

"What's happened to Mark?" Yale demanded, suddenly concerned.

"He got a steer horn in his breastbone this morning." Duel smiled. "It's why Mark sent for you. They brought him to town in a wagon. He's spittin' blood. He won't last the night."

"You don't seem a damned bit concerned that your brother's hurt."

"The only thing that needs concern you, is my offer to buy you out."

"I'm not a man to be pushed," Yale warned.

The yellow gaze dropped to Yale's gunless belt. "If you're not a man to be pushed, you better go and see if Jake Byerly can fix you up with a pistol of some kind. A sort of lady's gun, maybe."

Insolently Duel Ashfork turned his back and elbowed his way into the saloon, where Yale glimpsed a mud ceiling and rows of bottles behind a plank bar.

Frowning, Yale continued up the steep walk. Nothing had changed with the passing of years. He'd spent his teens in the bloody era of border wars. And later, after seeing a runaway slave doused with coal-oil and set afire by a flung torch, he accepted the Union's cause at his own.

Coming along the street, that had once been a trail for the Spanish, a group of riders swung left toward Muldoon Alley. One of them, a huge man, black hat cuffed back on a shaved skull, was Charlie Santo, segundo at the Ashfork Rafter A.

Santo, seeing Yale on the walk, said loudly, "Why there's that Yankee man. Got his legs back again."

"I thought there was a dead hoss smell in the air," another laughed.

"I don't figure it was no ambusher that shot him," Santo said, grinning. "The blue-belly just tripped over his own gun."

Yale felt his cheeks flame, but he kept his mouth shut.

8

A white aproned clerk, washing the front window of the Rincon Emporium, seemed amused by the exchange.

When Yale climbed to the veranda of the Gadsen House he was met by Sheriff Josh Wheatley. "Couldn't help but overhear, Yale. But don't take it to heart. With Duel back and Mark bad hurt, the Rafter A boys are just letting off a little steam."

"I've seen men killed for letting off that kind of steam," Yale said shortly.

Wheatley pursed his lips. He was a tall, spare man, graying now. In his fifties, a man who had prospered with the town of Rincon, living with his daughter Thela in a large house on the slope above Mesilla Street. He favored suits with a Frisco cut, and despite his glib politician manner, could be tough enough when the occasion demanded.

"Duel's not a bad sort," Yale's future father-in-law said confidentially. "Don't let all this talk about the range blowing up panic you."

"Josh, most of my life I've lived in country that was either blowing up or about to. I'm not panicked. I'm just damned sick of smelling burned powder and counting the dead."

Wheatley rubbed at his bristly mustache and gave Yale a speculative look out of amber eyes. "One thing to learn early in life, if a man wants to live to be a success—let the other fella smell the powder and count the dead."

Yale started to say that a man with such a philosophy was hardly one to take on the job of sheriff in such rough country.

He said, "I'm surprised the Mexicans didn't shoot Duel. I understand he killed one of their generals."

"The kind of general Duel put under isn't hard come by in that country. The Mexes kept waiting for Mark to send money—"

"How badly is Mark hurt?"

"A dyin' kind of hurt, so Mark seems to think. If you got any business with him, you better hurry it up." Wheatley paused, waiting for Yale to divulge any dealings he might have with Mark Ashfork. But Yale didn't take the bait. Clearing his throat, the sheriff said, "Too bad we haven't had a doc here since Adams died. A good one might be able to save Mark."

"I'm thankful Doc Adams lived long enough to save my hide, anyway."

"Thela's expecting you to take supper with us tonight."

9

"I haven't forgotten." Yale looked through the lobby windows, seeing some men grouped around the door to Mark Ashfork's room. "How did an old cowhand like Mark happen to get himself gored?"

"Even an Ashfork oughta know better than to be afoot when he argues with a bull." Wheatley put a hand on Yale's arm. "Mind what I said about Duel."

"I know. You said he isn't a bad sort."

Wheatley looked affronted. "I'm very close to Rafter A. I know what I'm talking about. Mark and Duel never got along, and now Duel's got a chance to be a big man himself, with this new herd he brought with him."

"Rustled from the Mexicans. Duel the same as admitted it."

"Since when's stealing from a Mexican any crime?" Wheatley gave his belly-shaking politician's laugh. When Yale failed to join him, the sheriff sobered. "I see you haven't forgot the time we hung the Mex hoss thief."

"See you tonight, Josh."

Yale walked into the hotel. Ludlow Carter came out of his office behind the desk. "Glad you got here, Braden. Mark Ashfork's been asking for you."

Yale nodded to the narrow face with its steel-rimmed spectacles. As he moved across the lobby, Carter whispered loudly, "What do you think of Duel coming home with all those cows?"

"It'll probably change a lot of lives hereabouts." And Yale wanted to add: But it won't change mine.

In California, he thought, a man and his bride could make a niche for themselves and not have to defend it with artillery.

10

CHAPTER TWO

The door to the room that Mark Ashfork rented by the year had been branded with his own hot iron, Rafter A. The men in the hall, talking in low tones, broke off as Yale appeared. He noted a sprinkling of merchants and some reps from the other big cattle outfits south of Rafter A. Two of the group acknowledged Yale's presence, but the others ignored him.

Seated in a propped up chair, shotgun across his knees, was Pop Grimsby, the Rafter A cook. Some said this narrow-eyed old man was stone deaf. Others said he just pretended to be. Grimsby leaned forward to peer at Yale. Satisfied with his identity he reached around and opened the door.

Yale closed the heavy door behind him, shutting off the faces of the curious in the hall. Ashfork lay in an oversize bed. He had his younger brother's height, but there was about him a suggestion of the probable size of the bull that had gored him. The room was spacious, with desk, chairs and Indian rugs on the floor. The shade of a copper lamp held a high polish.

"Took you long enough to get here," Mark Ashfork muttered. Usually the rancher shouted. Yale crossed over to the bed, noting the grayness at Mark's lips, a fever flush at the weathered brow. The bandage covering the wide chest was sweated and stained with blood.

"Mark, I'm sorry to see you this way."

"When a man's lived half a century, it's time he let the others do the rough work. I got careless." His eyes turned bitter. "Maybe it was Duel comin' home that had me thinkin' about—other things."

"He made me an offer for my place."

"I hope you spit on him."

Mark Ashfork's gray hair, atop his ruggedly handsome face, was neatly combed. A deep scar ran diagonally across the right side of his throat, made, some said, by a Comanche war lance in Texas.

Ashfork, propped up on pillows, watched him narrowly.

"Hope I don't look as bad as you did. When I packed you to town last year with that hole in your back."

"I've told you repeatedly that I appreciate what you did. I've tried to be friends, but you didn't want it that way. If there's anything I can do to repay—"

"Repay! That's the word I want to hear." A shred of the old powerful voice exploded in the room. "There comes a time in life when a man pays his debts. Or he isn't a man."

Yale straddled a chair and said carefully, "What is it you want of me?"

Ashfork wiped his lips on a bandanna. Some said that Mark Ashfork was the richest man in this corner of the territory. Mark never denied it. After the establishment of Abilene as a shipping point for the Texas drovers, the Ashforks had concentrated their holdings in New Mexico.

"Braden, you figure to tuck tail and run? Or stay and fight?"

"Fight who, and for what?"

"When I'm dead Duel will try to take over Rafter A. He'll try and ride you down along with the hill crowd."

"Maybe you won't die. They say you can do about anything you set your mind to."

"A man knows when his time comes." The leonine head turned on the pillow. Brown eyes, flecked with yellow, studied Yale. "You want to sell out?"

"Yes. You asked me to give you first chance if I ever planned to sell. And I intended seeing you about it—"

"Duel comin' back sorta decided you, huh?"

"I'd been considering it long before your brother returned home."

"Still figure to marry Thela?"

Yale flushed, "I plan our future in California. But we'll be married here, of course."

Mark Ashfork stared at the ceiling. "Duel courted her for a time. Before you come here."

"I didn't know that."

"Surprised, huh?"

"Are you still offering the agreed price for my ranch?"

The sun had shifted in the window and the lamp shade lost its shine. Horsemen swinging along the alley lifted dust against the pane.

Ashfork stirred on the bed. "You owe me a debt. I also owe. When I come here in Sixty-seven, the 'Paches were out and wide-loopers ran a man crazy. Mistakes were made.

12

One time I done wrong by a man named Ron Channa. He once ranched this whole valley."

"What has this to do with me?"

"Channa's sister and her no-account husband got a raggedy-pants outfit south of here. It's Ron Channa's daughter I owe the debt to. She lives with them. You know her?"

"I've seen the girl."

"A real beauty. Proud. I want to do something fine for her before I die."

"She'll be glad to hear it, I'm sure. Now about the ranch—"

"You'll be the one to tell her."

"Me? Tell her what?"

"That I want to get squared away. I aim to marry that girl. On my deathbed."

Yale drummed fingers on the back of the chair he straddled. Through the window he could see a bull team pulling a freight wagon and trailer. "What good will it do the Channa girl to marry her? You say you'll be dead."

"She'll be my widow. I own Rafter A, Duel don't. But I reckon most everybody has guessed as much by this time." Mark pushed a shaking hand under the bedclothes. He tried to draw out a large goatskin bag with heavy stitching at the seams. But he lacked the strength to move it. He tapped the bag, eying Yale. "Twenty thousand in that bag, Braden. In gold."

"The price we agreed on, if I ever decided to sell—"

"I'll double it. Forty thousand. If you make sure the Channa girl takes over at Rafter A when I'm dead. She'll be my widow and you'll be my foreman."

"You already have a foreman."

"Cliff DeLong is Duel's man, not mine. DeLong's a killer. And there are times when you need that kind. But layin' here with hell's door half open, I been thinkin'. DeLong's never been my man. Not even when Duel was in that Mex prison."

Yale stared at the big man on the bed, crudely bandaged. Dying, he claimed.

"That sort of proposition is out of my line," Yale told him.

"Mule shidd. You got some people fooled, Braden. But I know you. Down deep I know you. You're a tough man."

"My experience has proved that the tough ones have short lives."

Mark, watching him, said, "That wound still itch?"

"On occasion," and instinctively Yale reached around to feel an indentation to one side of the right armpit.

"You're lucky to have your life and be able to feel that itch. It's more than I'll have soon."

"You're too stubborn to die. Have you sent to Mesilla for a doctor—"

"No. I been shot at, hacked, stabbed, clubbed. But now I swung my last loop, busted my last ca'tridge." The yellow-flecked gaze drilled into Yale's face. "Fetch the Channa girl here. I already got a preacher in tow—I'll marry her right in this room, then die in peace."

"You could send Duel for her."

"That snake isn't fit to breathe the same air as Lucinda Channa." Mark Ashfork's voice was weaker, his color bad. "Your word, Braden, that you'll fetch the girl."

"She won't listen to me—"

"Ah, but she will." Ashfork closed his eyes a moment. "One time when you first settled here, some folks in the Emporium were draggin' your name through the mud with long ropes. And Lucinda Channa spoke up and said that she admired you for trying to make us like you. Especially former Texians who got a reason to hate you double."

"You mean Texas memories go back to the Missouri days. Your brother already reminded me today."

"That and the fact you fought Nawth. But this girl says that you had more gumption than the lot of 'em. She said you were a man of peace and this country was the better for you settlin' here. And that you shamed the lot of us because you could live your life without wearin' a gun."

"I didn't realize she even knew I was on this earth."

"Oh, she set some store by you, Braden. She said you read books. That you was a teacher once."

"It seems," Yale said dryly, "that there are no secrets in this country."

"She'll listen to you, Braden. You speak up for me real good, you hear?"

"It's a lot to ask of a man."

"Braden, there was a time if I seen you layin' in that trail, pumping your life's blood, I'd have just rode on. And to hell with you. But I fetched you to town and the doc saved your life."

Yale took a deep breath, then got up from the rawhide slatted chair. "I'll give this Channa girl your proposition."

"I knew you would. Forty thousand can stir the blood of most any man."

14

"If she's greedy enough to marry you, then she's capable of hiring her own killers. She can't hire me to see that she sits an easy saddle when you're gone."

Mark Ashfork's mouth turned ugly and he half-raised himself from the bed. But the effort cost him. He fell back, his mouth opening. Yale bent over him, thinking for an instant that the rancher was dead.

Then the eyes opened. "You're a damn fool, Braden," he said, his voice hushed, angry. "Forty thousand is more money than—" He broke off. "You're stubborn as me, ain't you? All right, fetch her here. Do your best for me with the girl. Your word, Braden."

Ashfork put out his hand. Yale took the hand. It was hot with fever. "There's no guarantee she'll agree," Yale reminded.

"Try, that's all I ask. When you fetch her you can write out the quit claim deed for your ranch." He made a feeble gesture toward the money bag on the bed. "The twenty thousand will be yours."

"I'll do my best."

"I carry a heavy cross on account of that girl," Mark Ashfork said heavily. *A cross of rope.*"

"What does that mean?"

"Never mind." Then, sick as he was, Mark Ashfork drew from beneath the blankets a long-barreled pistol. "And in case you figure to maybe sneak back and steal the twenty thousand—"

Yale stiffened. "I'm not a thief."

Ashfork let down the hammer of his revolver. "No, reckon you ain't. That's the brand my goddam brother wears."

When Yale went out into the hall he saw the men there look at him inquiringly. But Yale stepped around them without speaking. Grimsby still sat his chair, guarding the door with a shotgun.

In the lobby Duel Ashfork heaved himself out of a chair. He blocked the door to the veranda.

"What'd Mark want with you?" Duel demanded.

"It was a confidential matter." Yale's mouth hardened. "I've given considerable thought to the identity of my ambusher. The name Cliff DeLong has been crossing my mind. Did you suggest he try and kill me?"

"I was in Mexico. And why, after all this time, do you wonder about our foreman?"

"Something Mark said today. About DeLong being your man. DeLong never being Mark's man. Maybe you got word

15

to him somehow from the prison, when you heard how things were here."

Duel tipped back his hat, gave him an insolent smile. "You mean Thela?"

"You used to court her. Something nobody ever bothered to tell me until today."

Yale brushed past the younger Ashfork brother and stalked on down to the livery for his horse. It would be a long ride to Pete Hatcher's raggedy-pants outfit.

Five miles or so east of town he crossed the Mesilla road, skirting the Half Pine way station, a dun-colored building with corrals, on the stage route. The slashed tree that had given the place its name loomed against the sky like a stubby forefinger.

Some miles below the way station he passed a large herd of cattle guarded by a group of slender, hard-eyed men in big hats. They held rifles, watching him. Some of them, Yale noted, rode Rafter A horses.

Probably the vaqueros and the cattle Duel Ashfork had brought back with him from Mexico.

Yale lifted a hand to them, but kept out of their way and at last came to the great tablelands where the Hatcher place lay like a scabrous knob on the face of the land.

CHAPTER THREE

When Yale Braden had taken his leave Mark Ashfork closed his eyes; the inside of the lids were on fire. The talk with the 88 owner had drained him. Damn it, why had Braden argued with him? Why hadn't Braden agreed to pay his debt and shut up about it? As he tried to turn on his side he felt a great hot wire drawn through his chest, that caused a grunt of pain to escape his lips. He lay, bathed in cold sweat, hoping to God that Braden rode a fast horse and caught up a fresh one at Pete Hatcher's place to get the girl back in time.

He knew Braden could do it. Braden might have been short on sense when it came to choosing sides in the war, and worrying about Texas fever afterwards, but he had made a paying proposition out of 88 after he took over from that fool Englishman.

For one of the few times in his life, he mumbled a prayer: "God, give me strength to hang on till I right this wrong."

For forty-six of his fifty years the righting of wrongs was something that had never concerned Mark. Then, five years ago in '68, something happened that evoked a mighty change in him. It was in this very bed. The night he learned the thing with Ron Channa had been irrevocably settled by Cliff DeLong and some of the Rafter A men.

That night, when he had heard the news, he drank whisky at Quincy's and Sheriff Josh Wheatley, among others, had said, "I say good riddance to Channa. . ." Later, when the whisky had thickened Mark Ashfork's head, he remembered Wheatley saying, "About that Channa house here in town, Mark. It would be a fine place to raise my daughter."

No matter how drunk he might be, Mark never forgot what was said to him. He told Wheatley he would sign over the house to him. After all, the Ashforks had been buying sheriffs for years. This one wanted a house. Well, why not?

Mark had staggered up to bed and old Grimsby had laid aside his shotgun long enough to help Mark off with his boots. Grimsby blew out the lamp and padded out.

Then, lying in the bed, Mark had seen someone at the foot. At first he thought it was Grimsby come back in the dark to write out a message for him, as was his custom. But it wasn't Grimsby.

It was Momma.

She stood right there, her big gnarled hands gripping the foot of the bed. Her hair wild as he remembered when he was little. Her voice so loud, some said, it could be heard forty miles south along the Rio from their place in Texas.

"You done wrong, Mark!" she screamed at him, her eyes fierce. "You're a wicked man."

"Momma, it's so good to hear your voice."

"Mend your ways, Mark. Mend your ways. Or you'll burn. Through all eternity you'll burn!"

"Listen to me, Momma—"

"Start paying your debts, Mark. Undo the wrongs—"

There was a pounding on the door, and Ludlow Carter stood there, holding a lamp and a pistol. Men crowding in behind the bespectacled owner of the Gadsen House. And Mark Ashfork reared up in the bed, shouting, "What in hell you mean coming in here like this?"

"I used the spare key!" Carter was looking wildly around at the shadows in the big room not reached by the lamp. "I swear to God I thought somebody was murdering you."

"I was sound asleep."

One of the men, Ardin Southworth of the Rincon Hardware, put his flushed, plump face in the doorway. "You were shouting, Mark. Honest to God!"

"Nightmare," somebody else offered.

"Clear out!" Mark Ashfork shouted, and when they had gone he took a long drink from his bottle and went back to sleep. Momma did not appear again. But she had left her message.

He started to mend his ways, all right. Word got around that Mark Ashfork wasn't as tough as he used to be. And it was rumored that as a consequence some members of his crew were getting a little hard to handle.

Once he tried to speak to Lucinda Channa when he saw her on the street, but the yellow-haired beauty stared at him coldly and walked on, her head high. He would leave her money when he died. But that would be *after* he was gone. He wanted to do something before he died.

But the matter was pushed from his mind by the numerous emergencies that beset a rancher trying to hold his empire in

18

such country. 'Paches had come twice in one year and the cattle and horses they couldn't run off, they killed.

Then, last year, Mark was coming back from a confab with old Jeremiah Peters. He had told the old bandit that he would meet with him and it was agreed. And Mark Ashfork told Peters to stay in the hills and Rafter A would leave them alone.

"Duel's in a Mex prison," Mark told the bearded head of the clan. "So he won't bother you none. And he can rot there, for all I care."

He had shaken hands with Jeremiah Peters (Uncle Jer to his kinsmen), and ridden back toward Rincon. Halfway through the mountains he heard a rifle shot. And a little later his horse shied at something lying in the trail. It was Yale Braden, face down, an ugly wound in his back.

It was twenty miles to Rincon and he packed the man all that way. Mark hoped that his mother, wherever she might be, was somehow aware of what he had done. Not only helped mend his ways by saving a life, but a blue-belly life. That sure made up for a lot.

Not that he was particularly superstitious, but his mother had had a powerful influence on him in those wild days after his father died for the glory of Texas and Sam Houston. The younger Ashfork boys—all dead now, save Duel—were not so much a part of the struggle as was Mark. One lone, dominant woman, holding out on the frontier with a passel of young sons. It was only in her last year that she took to reading Scripture. She said that everybody does bad things in his lifetime—things you have to right before you die.

One thing she regretted most was the time at sundown when she mistook the drunken Mexican for a Comanche. She and Mark buried him behind the barn.

Mark felt of the bandage on his chest. The pain was steady now and he only hoped when Lucinda Channa entered this room, he had strength enough left to show her he was sorry about her father.

"Paying my debt," he would tell her. "Rafter A, all yours. Everything. You can hire an army to protect you—"

He fell asleep with fever riding him down long canyons where his mother shouted at him, and he could see again the war lance stabbing for his throat when he was young. And he remembered the redman who had tried to kill him, shot in the guts with Mark's own pistol. And the war lance only put a deep scar along his neck.

Pop Grimsby, who had been called Tex in his younger days, came in to peer at Mark. The old man laid the back of a hand on the burning face. Shaking his head, Grimsby went out and resumed his post, the shotgun in his lap.

CHAPTER FOUR

Down through the dun-colored hills rode Yale Braden. Spring color flashed. Ahead, he could see the Hatcher place. Weeks ago he had ridden here for the first time when Pete Hatcher, Lucinda Channa's uncle, had some horses to sell. But after looking them over Yale had decided against buying. That day he'd had a glimpse of Lucy Channa with her bright hair and straight back. She was somehow incongruously regal in the grubby surroundings. He knew the Channas had once been a power, but whenever he asked about it, people changed the subject. For some reason they seemed to think discussion of the Channas offended Mark Ashfork. And to offend an Ashfork was something no sane person did on the Rincon range.

When he dismounted in the weed-grown yard Yale waved to some children, three girls and five boys, who streamed out of one of the small 'dobe houses, a little to the south of the main house. They shouted to him, laughing. But three gaunt young women, wearing shawls, came to the yard and called sharply to the children. The children quieted, and the women stared across the yard at Yale, offering no word of greeting.

Hatcher, a stringy man, rifle under his arm, appeared on the porch of the largest of the sod roofed structures. He came up to Yale, his eyes bright and speculative in a narrow, unshaven face.

"So you come back about them hosses. Can make you a fair price."

"I have a message for your niece, Lucinda."

Hatcher studied him a moment, rubbing a hand over the front of his patched, sweat-marked shirt. "You give me the message. I'll pass it along."

"It's a private matter."

A voice from the house called, "What is it, Uncle Pete?"

Lucinda Channa was coming down the veranda steps, wearing a green cotton dress. The other times he'd seen her she wore canvas jeans and boots. Today her plaited hair was pinned up. And somehow the way she lifted her skirts, the stately manner in which she made her way across

21

the yard through a collection of squawking hens made Yale think of a ballroom. Even the dust and manure smell, the barking of a dog, the staring children and the gaunt, older women, did not dispel his feeling that she was a beautiful girl walking across a polished floor with candlelight touching cut glass, and an orchestra playing. She caught him staring at her, and he flushed, feeling like a fool.

"I know you," she said in a deeply pleasant voice. "The college professor from Missouri."

"Only briefly, I'm afraid. After the war, in Missouri, at least, a teacher was hard put. Nobody wanted to learn. All they wanted," he went on bitterly, "was to talk of the rebellion."

She caught her full underlip in her teeth. They were very white. Her eyes very blue in an intelligent face. "You could have gone somewhere else to teach."

"I'm afraid this isn't the age for it. I'm a businessman now. I find it offers a great deal more than the other." The flush deepened on his face, this time in anger not embarrassment, that he found it necessary to explain his actions to this girl.

"You disappoint me." Her lashes were long under pale brows. "I understand you're Thela Wheatley's betrothed."

"Yes. You know her?"

"We were friends—once."

Pete Hatcher said, "Lucy, he's got a message for you."

"From Mark Ashfork," Yale put in.

Lucinda Channa stared at him for a moment, her eyes shocked. "I find myself completely disinterested in any message from Mark Ashfork."

Lifting her skirts, she started back to the house. But Yale took a long step forward, and caught her by the arm. He was aware of firm warm flesh under his fingers. For a moment he let his hand remain on her arm as if afraid to break contact with her. At first her eyes were startled as she looked around at him. Then he saw the steel lights in them.

Yale dropped his hand. "Miss Channa, I'm sorry. But—"

Hatcher was scowling at his niece. "Won't do no harm to hear what Ashfork—"

"Haven't the Ashfork's done enough already!" she cried.

"Mark Ashfork may be dying," Yale told her. "He wants to make amends."

"Make amends? In what way?" Her mouth trembled. "By

22

saying he's sorry he ordered my father hanged like a common thief?"

Yale stood woodenly. Silence thickened across the yard, broken only by the chattering hens. "I—I didn't know that about your father."

Hatcher was thumbing his stubbly jaw. "Does Mark figure to settle some money on her, maybe?"

"I think I'd better tell Miss Channa in private."

The girl had regained some of her color. "You can speak in front of my uncle."

Yale debated a moment. "Very well. Mark wants to marry you."

She stared incredulously. Then a peal of shaky laughter was torn from her throat. "Marry *me*! Are you serious?"

Greed rose like a flag across Hatcher's eyes. "Braden, is this some trick of Duel's? I hear he's back—"

"The offer is genuine."

"Why would Mark send you?" Hatcher demanded.

"I'm indebted to him."

Lucy Channa said, "Oh, yes. I remember. Mark brought you to town when you were shot."

"Isn't that reason enough to try and repay a man?" Yale felt an edge to his voice. "What more could you owe than your very life?"

She took a deep breath, swelling the front of her dress. "You've delivered your message, Mr. Braden. Now you can go—"

Pete Hatcher cried, "Now just a minute there!" Cupping his hands, he shouted at the main house. "Martha, get on out here!"

Hatcher's wife, munching a piece of cake, waddled across the yard on her fat legs. Hatcher made Yale tell the story again.

"A deathbed ceremony, is all Mark Ashfork expects," Yale finished. "Your niece will be his widow. His heir."

"*Ai—ai—ai—*!" Hatcher cried, in the manner of an exuberant Mexican, banging his hat on a bony knee. "Mrs. Mark Ashfork. I kinda like the sound of it, Lucy."

"I don't," Lucinda Channa declared. "I've had quite enough of this nonsense."

When Hatcher started to berate her, Yale said quietly, "It's her decision. Not yours."

"She owes us something. Me an' Martha took her in—"

"Pete's right," Martha Hatcher said, wiping crumbs from

23

her soft chin. "If everything is as Braden says, Lucy, you'll just let a preacher say a few words. And you'll have Mark's money. Isn't that worth thinking about—"

"No. It isn't worth thinking about."

"But, honey—" Martha Hatcher broke off, looking perplexed, turning to her husband for guidance. She had evidently once been attractive, but now seemed to take her pleasure or escape in eating. Her figure strained the seams of a cheap dress. A strand of graying hair had curled on the sweated surface of her flabby throat.

"The Ashfork name would be something to consider," Hatcher said eagerly.

"The Ashfork name would bring no pride to me," the girl stated flatly.

"If Mark is dying like Braden claims, then there isn't much time." Excitement ran through Hatcher's voice like a humming wire. "This is a day for paying debts, Lucy. Braden is paying his to Ashfork. You should pay yours to me and Martha and your cousins."

Tears pushed at the girl's lashes. She looked at Yale. "Thank you for coming, Mr. Braden."

Hatcher's enraged gaze swung from his niece to Braden. "Ain't you going to argue with her, Braden? You could talk fancy and show her she owes it to her kin—"

"As I said. It's her decision. Hers alone." Yale stood deepening the crease in his hat. Now he put it on his head, touched the brim. "Miss Channa, I've delivered a message. Evidently you prefer to turn down this offer. Can't say I blame you."

When he swung into the saddle Hatcher was whispering angrily to the girl. And when she just stood, white-faced, ignoring him, her eyes on Yale, he exploded.

"You could be a better persuader than you are!" Hatcher stormed at Yale. And when Yale said nothing, Hatcher's gaze fastened on Yale's belt, finding an object to scorn. "Seein' as how you was shot at once, I'd think you'd take to wearin' a gun."

Yale touched the butt of a booted rifle. "This is sufficient for my needs."

"Comes a time when a short gun up close is the only medicine—"

"Leave him alone, Uncle Pete." Lucinda turned on her uncle. "Can't you see he's a man of peace. And—and I admire him for it."

24

Whirling, she dashed for the house.

Yale sat his saddle a moment feeling a sudden warmth, as if something nice had happened to him for a change. Then, touching his hat to Martha Hatcher, he rode out.

CHAPTER FIVE

A man of peace. Yale wanted to laugh. For most of his life he had been a party to the constant improvements in the methods of killing other human beings. The final refinements had come during the war. Although he had a cavalryman's carriage, it had been artillery that claimed him.

The refinements of warfare were much greater in artillery. You did not necessarily see your victims. Not until the following day if you were fortunate enough to advance. Then you saw the broken bodies, the smashed houses, the dead horses. This was impersonal fighting.

He'd started with Napoleon howitzers. Load with a twelve pound ball and with luck it would carry just short of a mile. His next taste of leadership had been with Parrott Rifles that could blast an eighty pound shot over four miles, when elevated to an angle of thirty-five degrees. This was impersonal —impersonal. From five miles away you scarcely need give a thought to whom you might kill.

Occasionally he had been called upon to engage in direct slaughter. Then his Parrott Rifles were fired point blank at advancing cavalry, with men and animals raked across the bloodied ground.

It was late when he reached Rincon. Some of the Rafter A men were guarding Mark Ashfork's door. They said Mark was asleep and could not be awakened under any circumstances.

Leader of the group was a red-bearded man named Eddie Toll. Yale said, "Tell Mark that I was here. Tell him the answer is no."

"Answer to what?" Toll demanded coldly.

"He'll understand."

As he came out of the hotel he felt vaguely depressed and realized he should have taken the evening meal with Thela and her father. But they would have retired at this hour. He sensed Thela would make him pay for his oversight.

As he tiredly rode for home he could not help but think of Lucinda and how her life might have differed, had not

26

the Ashforks decided to settle in New Mexico. And this brought his own past into focus and the imponderables that had changed his life. Enlisting at eighteen he had been elected lieutenant at twenty by his company of Missouri Volunteers. After the war he had returned to Southern Missouri, seeing the results of a blight called Quantrell. His older brother, Bish, had been barely able to hold things together during the conflict; the lumber mill, the store, the ranch.

Yale had started his own career, teaching at the Ashville Academy, but that was short-lived. The following year came the Texas drovers, for the Missouri-Pacific had pushed south to Sedalia, affording rail lines to St. Louis and other beef markets. Some of the first herds brought Texas fever, and the Bradens and their neighbors lost many head of cattle to the disease. The Texas herds were turned back at the Missouri border. Later, in a gunfight, Yale's brother was killed.

Yale had sold out and come to New Mexico because here he believed a man could run his life without aligning himself with one faction or the other. He believed that here the war was over and forgotten. He had purchased 88 through a dealer in Mesilla.

He soon realized that here he was disliked on two counts in some quarters; first, he had fought for the North and second, his name. And the name was connected with those elements, good or bad, depending on the viewpoint, that had forced drovers to bypass Missouri and seek a new railhead for their herds. These had been bloody years, for even though the original complaint had been genuine—the infecting of Missouri cattle by Texas fever—others took advantage of the situation. Outlaws moved in and small town politicians demanded tribute from the Texans. It was a time for appropriating herds by one means or another. And around Texas campfires Southern Missouri became a name to curse.

Yale Braden had been raised during the feverish years of abolitionist against slavery. He had seen his father shot down, his uncle dragged behind a horse because a runaway slave had been sheltered.

Now here in New Mexico he had found that bloodshed was a cloak he could not easily discard. During his second year on 88 an ambusher had shot him in the back and left him for dead. Fortunately the ball had gone clear through his body or no surgeon could have saved him.

It was Sheriff Wheatley's opinion that the shot had likely come from the rifle of a renegade who was after Yale's horse and purse. And then was frightened off when Mark Ashfork rode up. Wheatley had followed horse tracks with a posse, but lost the sign deep in the Mogollons. And that was the end of it. . . .

With a moon rising he sighted his 88 at the foot of the mountains. Unpainted outbuildings silvered by moonlight. He splashed across Victoria Creek, renamed from the Spanish by the Englishman who had formerly owned the spread. No lights showed from the buildings he could see through cottonwoods and aspens. He'd had a good calf crop this year and it was cause for celebration. But he felt empty.

Old habits, learned on the bloody Missouri border, had taught him to avoid the silent approach unless you planned an attack. So he came up noisily toward the bunkhouse.

Bill Striker stepped out and cautioned someone, "Don't light a lamp till we know who it is."

"Yale Braden!" Yale said loudly.

"Still no lights," Striker ordered.

Yale swung down. "What's happened here, Bill?"

Striker came up, tall, rangy, rifle under his arm. "You know that black hoss you figured to break to saddle?"

"Yes. I take some pride in it. Why do you ask."

"Somebody shot it this evening." And as Yale felt a shaft of ice move up from his creek-soaked pants to his spine, Striker held out a knife and a crumpled square of paper. "This note was pinned to the hoss with the knife."

Angered, Yale stepped to the bunkhouse and touched a match to a lamp wick. He could see the crew watching him from their bunks.

Printed in square black letters on a dirty piece of paper was a message. GO BACK TO MISSOURI. Yale felt color drain from his face.

"What in hell is the meaning of this, Bill?"

"It means somebody wants you to get out. What else?"

Striker told how just after sunset they had heard a rifle shot in the south pasture. They had ridden over and found the dead horse and the note. They'd followed tracks for a ways but lost them when the horse killer moved down the creek.

Yale managed to hold onto his slipping temper. Striker watched him as if waiting for a verbal explosion against whoever had committed this despicable act. The bunkhouse smelled of dust and old grease from the adjoining cookshack.

Yale's jaws were tightly locked as he examined the knife.

28

It was a clasp knife with a pearl handle. He dropped it into his pocket. He'd have to find another birthday present for Thela.

"He would have been a good saddler," Yale said.

He swung up the path to his own house while one of the men cared for his mount. He knew Striker was disappointed in him. Tonight's happening intensified his determination to clear out. Sleep was hard come by.

CHAPTER SIX

Lucinda Channa sat in a small chair. The chair was old, reinforced at the rungs by rawhide. Her hands folded in her lap, she watched the parade of her relatives in the lamplight. Uncle Pete occupied the center of the long, drab room with the stove and stone fireplace taking up one end. Beyond was her room and that of Uncle Pete and Aunt Martha. Her aunt was staring at her hopefully, a half-smile on her lips. It was sometimes hard for Lucinda to realize that this was her blood kin, this mountainous woman who was sister to her dead father. Married to a greedy shank of a man named Pete Hatcher. Her father, Lucinda recalled, had been against the match. Pete Hatcher was a shiftless cowhand, fairly presentable fifteen years ago when Lucinda was seven. Her father had helped him take up sections southeast of Rincon, and that was where they lived now.

Pete Hatcher had lined her three shirttail kin, as they were called in this country, across the room. The three Channa women, all under thirty, were gaunt, bitter women in faded cotton with the stamp of widowhood in their tight mouths. Rose and Belle and Kate. Once they had been young, their faces full, expecting life to give them much. Life had given them children. It had taken away everything else.

Uncle Pete led Kate, the oldest, to the center of the room. "Look at her, Lucy. She was married to your brother. Bob was—"

"Stop it!" Lucinda cried, getting up. "I know the Ashforks had him shot. You don't have to remind me."

"In a card game at Rincon. Crooked cards, Charlie Santo claimed. He shot Bob in the head and—" Hatcher gestured at three of the young boys. They moved up beside their mother. "These here younguns got no father on account of Rafter A."

Lucinda sat down and buried her face in her hands. The bloody years unreeled again before her eyes. Her own father, lovable, but incompetent. Gambling, drinking. Not the steel of the grandfather. In '67 the Ashforks came and they decided the Channa land should be theirs. A little of it went

30

here and there. Until the final smashing blow. The death of her father. Hanged like a thief.

And no one had protested. Oh, some were shocked, privately. Even Josh Wheatley had come by and removed his hat and said, "I'm right sorry about your father. But—well, these are bad times."

Bad times.

Pete Hatcher said, "And here's Rose and Belle, married to your cousins, Lucy. No father for their kids either. On account of the Ashforks."

Lucinda listened to the reedy voice drone on, interrupted occasionally by her aunt's hasty interjections concerning duty.

Lucy, you owe us.

You owe Kate and Rose and Belle.

You owe, you owe, you owe.

The word burned into her brain like hot irons. She felt a flash of tears. The one man who had come here who had Grandfather Channa's steel—Yale Braden. A man who had fought for the Union and who allowed people to say words behind his back, such as blue-belly, without lifting a hand to them. And yet even these people learned however grudgingly, to respect him. This man she would see on the streets of Rincon. This man who stirred a small inner trembling the few times he had lifted his hat to her, this man betrothed to Thela Wheatley.

Oh, God, is there no justice at all? With Duel home, won't things go on as before? And will Thela's fickle heart hurt this Yale Braden irreparably? Or does Josh realize at last that Duel is penniless. That Mark owns Rafter A?

But then Duel had come home with a herd of Mexican cattle. Josh Wheatley might weigh the two—Yale Braden against two thousand head of cows.

What did it matter, really? she told herself. She was tired, tired. They would kill Yale Braden. He did not know it but he was doomed, as her father had been doomed.

She put her hands over her ears to drown out the voice of her uncle; a voice pleading one moment, snarling at her the next.

"Widows, orphans, Lucy. Your poor aunt and me. We give up much to help you, Lucy."

Rising, she looked her Uncle Pete in the eye. She wanted to say, My father supported you for years. Deny it if you can.

She said, her voice a little shrill, "If it will please you, I will consider marrying Mark Ashfork. Consider, mind you."

31

"Wheee—" Uncle Pete shouted, jumping up and down.

"But," Lucinda continued, "if I do marry him and he ever lives to take me to bed, I'll kill him!"

Turning on her heel, she walked to her room and slammed the door.

Pete Hatcher grinned at his wife. "I knew she'd do it if we kept at her long enough."

"A shocking thing for her to say," Martha Hatcher stated, glaring at the bedroom door. "Speaking that way in front of the children."

"We'll take her to Mark right away. And pray that he ain't dead. Pray like you never prayed before, Martha."

CHAPTER SEVEN

In the morning Yale took breakfast with his seven-man crew at the cookshack. The men seemed withdrawn, intent only on the food that the fat cook, Alex Beacham, put before them. But he would catch them eying him. Most of them were former Texans, and he had hoped to prove that he had enough strength of character to make these men respect him. But now he sensed their disapproval.

Larry Arthur, the youngest man on the crew, was a towhead who had lost his wife two summers back, before Yale took over here. Arthur said, "I'm right sorry about your hoss gettin' shot, Mr. Braden. Damn shame—"

Yale had no chance to answer. There was a rattle of hoofbeats. Striker, who was facing the door, said, "Rafter A has come to call." Striker turned to the crew. "Better get your guns unlimbered, boys."

Yale said, "When it comes to giving orders about the defense of this ranch, Bill, I'll be the one to give them."

Yale stepped outside. He had angered Bill Striker. Well, the hell with him, he thought. It was his responsibility not Striker's.

He tipped the brim of his hat against the early sun that glowed yellow through a cut in the Mogollons. There was the smell of fresh water in the air. A horse neighed in the fenced pasture beyond the barn.

Five of the approaching riders were regular Rafter A hands, the tough cold-eyed type of man the Ashforks liked to hire. Duel Ashfork, astride a bay horse, was riding beside the foreman, Cliff DeLong. The men drew rein and sat staring down at Yale.

"Is Mark still alive?" Yale asked to break the heavy silence.

"Alive and that's about all." Duel dismounted, his yellow eyes insolent. "I came for an answer to my offer."

"I intend selling this ranch to your brother, if he lives long enough. If not, then to any man who will pay my price."

Cliff DeLong had hooked a leg over the saddlehorn. "The

Yankee man talks right up, Duel." He gave a gummy, old man laugh. The foreman was just past thirty yet incongruously the lower part of his face as that of an old man. At a fight in a wood camp near Paso Del Norte, so the story went, a length of firewood had been rammed with such force against his mouth that every tooth was torn from his head, his jaws permanently scarred.

Yale glared at the foreman. "I'm getting a belly full of certain things around here." Directing his attention to Duel, he drew the bloodied piece of paper and the pearl-handled knife from his pocket. "Is this your idea of a warning?"

"Where'd you get that?" Duel demanded.

"Answer me. Is this your knife?"

No expression crossed Duel Ashfork's dark face as Yale told how the knife had pinned a warning note to the body of the horse.

Duel took a hitch at his gunbelt. "I don't go around shooting horses," he stated flatly.

From a corner of his eye, Yale caught DeLong winking at Charlie Santo, who loomed like a granite slab in the saddle.

DeLong said, "This Braden fella used to be a fightin' man, they tell me. But the war put yellow grits where his guts used to be."

Yale let the insult roll free, but his gaze narrowed. "Shooting a horse might be your way of doing things, DeLong."

"How you mean, Union man?" DeLong said softly.

"Shoot a man in the back when he rides alone. And later on kill the man's prize horse."

The pale gray in DeLong's eyes caught fire. "A man can talk up real good when he don't wear a gun."

Duel said, "Nobody around here likes you much, Braden. I'm remembering another Braden, outa Sedalia. Your brother, I hear. He was there when we took our first Texas herd nawth in Sixty-Six—"

"Those were bad times, I admit—"

"Your brother and some of them other Missouri bandits claimed our cows had Texas fever."

"So they did."

"Liar!"

"Don't be so free with a word like that," Yale warned, and heard a stirring of his men in the cookshack behind him. Easy, he cautioned himself. One wrong word and men can die here. It's up to you to prevent it.

Duel said, "We lost the herd and a couple of my good friends got shot."

"I'm interested in the present, not the past. Did you know I planned to make Thela a present of that horse?"

"Not until Cliff told me he heard it somewheres—" Duel broke off, shooting DeLong a glance. For a moment Duel looked puzzled, then he broke into a grin.

DeLong was smiling with the indented lower half of his face. As if to compensate for his ruined face, DeLong wore two revolvers. His black clothing also seemed a part of his attempt to impress the world with his toughness. A sort of funereal effect all around when a man stopped to consider DeLong's reputation.

From a corner of his eyes Yale noticed that his men had come out to the yard, rifles at the ready. It could become a bad moment.

Yale stepped back, ramming the warning note and the knife into his pocket. "If you want to discuss the sale of my ranch," he told Duel, "next time come alone. I don't intend to have this place turned into a battlefield. After I dispose of this place you can damn well do what you want with it, but until then—"

"So you don't like the offer I made," Duel said narrowly.

"You know the answer to that," Yale snapped.

Duel Ashfork gave him a thoughtful stare, then swung into the saddle. Charlie Santo, astride a Rafter A roan, leaned his big frame against the horn, his voice booming from the oversize body. "Hey, Striker," he called to Yale's foreman. "How come you draw pay from a blue-belly Union man?"

Striker spat, hefted his rifle. "Santo, you make one damn big target."

Santo laughed and joined the other Rafter A men who were wheeling back the way they had come.

Staying home this morning depressed Yale, but there was bookwork to be done. He saw Striker and two of the men ride out. He never interfered with Striker's job, for he realized the man knew more about running cattle in the New Mexican rough country than he did. His 88 was paying well and he felt he had invested the proceeds from the Missouri property to good advantage. And since the complete recovery from his wound, he considered himself in a position to offer Thela Wheatley a substantial, relatively comfortable life.

It was the first time that morning Thela had crossed his mind. And he suddenly remembered his obligation. He saddled up and rode to town.

Once again Yale tried to see Mark Ashfork at the Gadsen House, but the clerk said word had been left not to disturb the rancher.

Yale walked to the Wheatley residence. For a weekday, he observed, the town was crowded. Many of the extra roundup hands in town waiting to be paid off.

It was on Saturday nights that Mesilla Street really came alive. With the sound of fiddles and the stomping of boots; the squeal of girls from Maude Telfer's establishment over on Muldoon Alley.

Above Mesilla Street a once-ornate 'dobe house was spread in front of a stand of aspen. A crumbling wall enclosed a courtyard and flashing fountain. The double doors, cracked from weather, hung by rusted hinges.

He crossed the courtyard tiles that were tufted with weeds. Sheriff Wheatley answered his knock and said, half-joking, "Thela's some put out at you."

"I came to apologize."

Then Thela herself swept into the room, Pretending not to notice Yale she kissed her father's cheek. It seemed to Yale that she was inappropriately dressed for so early in the day. She wore a pale gown of blue satin with small silver stars at the neckline.

"Why, look who has honored us at last," she said, with mock surprise.

Yale tried to smile at the dark-haired beauty. "I'm sorry about last night, Thela—"

"Oh, then you did remember. But you considered it unimportant."

Sheriff Wheatley forced a laugh. "Walk softly when she's on the warpath, Yale. I've learned that from long experience."

Thela, her gray eyes hot, said, "Did you enjoy your visit with Miss Channa?"

"So that's it," Yale murmured.

"Miss Channa was of more importance than taking supper with us last night."

"Thela, it was unavoidable." He sat down at a cherrywood table where Josh Wheatley had been drinking coffee. He helped himself. For some reason he ran his hand over the smooth wood of the table that had once belonged to a family that had come here in Spanish days to build a fortress in the wilderness. Here they had stood against the Spanish and mined silver and ran uncounted head of cattle, but had fallen upon bad years. He wondered how many times Lucinda Channa had sat at this very table.

36

Thela leaned close so that he could catch the musky fragrance she liked. "Just why did you go to the Hatcher place?"

Yale glanced up at the flushed, pretty face. "You'll find out in time. For now I consider it a matter I can't discuss."

Josh Wheatley set down his cup. "One of Pete Hatcher's men was in town today. Came to visit a friend of his in jail. I overheard him mention that you were out there late yesterday afternoon."

It disturbed Yale a little that he could find no liking for Wheatley. After failing as store owner, miner and small-scale rancher, Wheatley seemed to have found a measure of success here in Rincon. Besides owning this house he was said to have an interest in other town holdings. His luck had changed upon being elected sheriff with the backing of Mark Ashfork and the other big outfits. He could be efficient enough when the occasion demanded it. Usually he worked on the job alone, hiring extra deputies when needed.

Yale tasted the coffee. It was too bitter for his liking. He suggested to Thela that they take a walk. But she said she was not dressed for it.

"However, I will allow you to take me to the courtyard," she said crisply.

Sharing a bench with her in the shade, Yale tried to make conversation. But she sat stiffly. Yale knew she was a girl who found it easy to show her disapproval. At times he was hard pressed to know exactly what it was he did that had annoyed her.

But he did owe her a lot. For she had insisted months ago, upon learning he had been shot, that he be brought to this house where he could have proper care. She had nursed him in his long fight against death. There were times when she exasperated him, but he loved her quite deeply and usually took her changing moods in stride. He found that today he could not quite ignore her pettiness.

He cleared his throat. "Have you ever considered living in California?"

She looked at him in surprise. "But the gold rush is over. There would be no point—"

"There's more to California than the panning of gold."

"Surely you're not serious." Her hoop earrings caught the sunlight, and put small fires across her cheeks. "This house is my home, Yale."

He tried to smile. "I would hardly have the time, nor the

patience to dismantle this house and freight it all the way to California."

"Yale, honey, don't ask me to give up this house."

"There are some things in life we are forced to give up. Whether we want to or not."

She jerked to her feet. "Now if you will excuse me, I have things to do." Angrily she hurried into the house, heels rapping on the tiles.

Yale felt his cheeks grow hot. Wheatley came out of the house. "Don't look so glum, Yale. Thela's like her mother was in many ways. You'll learn to adjust to it. The sheriff cleared his throat. "Walking downtown, Yale? I'll go with you, soon as I get my hat."

Wheatley turned back for the house, and Yale said, "I'd like to join you, Josh. But I have to stop off at Byerly's." Yale had no reason to visit the gunsmith, but he didn't feel like listening to Josh Wheatley all the way downtown. He told the sheriff he'd see him later.

As he started away he thought of how, when he had first come here, the sheriff and he had had their differences. Some Mexican horse thieves had hit a ranch west of Rincon. Yale had been in town that day and Wheatley asked him to ride with the posse. Because he knew it was expected of him, as a ranch owner, Yale agreed. Within a matter of miles they overtook the thieves and their band of stolen horses. One of them managed to get away. One was shot dead when his hands were not raised fast enough to suit a posse member. The third one was hanged on the spot.

Angered, Yale said he thought it was a brutal interpretation of justice, no matter what the circumstances. But the sheriff stated thinly that he believed in saving the county money wherever possible. Number One, Wheatley pointed out, you didn't waste the time of a circuit judge by having a trial for a horse thief. Secondly, it was doubly true if the culprit happened to be a Mexican.

Only later, when Thela had shown an interest in Yale had the sheriff thawed in his attitude toward the younger man.

These things ran through Yale's mind as he entered Byerly's gunshop.

CHAPTER EIGHT

Jake Byerly was a querulous, untidy man, who let his neck hair grow long so he could comb it forward over a bald scalp. When Yale entered he looked up irritably from his workbench where he was polishing the stock of a shotgun.

Byerly climbed to his feet, wiping at a smear of gun oil on his cheek. "Wondered if you'd ever get around to spendin' money with me," he grunted.

"I've got a rifle with a broken hammer," Yale said. "Intended to bring it in, but forgot it." From a corner of his eye he saw Josh Wheatley tramp on past the shop on his way to Mesilla Street.

Byerly said, "Looks like everybody is gettin' their artillery in shape now that Duel's back." Byerly gave him a sly look. "How's Thela these days?"

"In good health, thank you."

"Josh had hopes of marrying into the Ashfork family at one time. But then Duel had to go and get himself locked up in that Mex prison. Besides, Duel's got no claim on Rafter A. Reckon you're substantial enough for Josh now."

"I'm really flattered," Yale said dryly.

"Next time you're in town, bring that rifle in." Byerly followed Yale to the door. "By any chance you got a revolver that needs fixin'?"

"No."

"Well, I just wondered why you never carried a pistol like everybody else around here."

"I don't particularly care for the fashion that requires a man to go armed at all times."

Byerly gave a thin laugh. "Braden, you're a damn fool."

"That's entirely possible," Yale snapped. He had the feeling he'd come off second best with Byerly.

As he walked out of the shop he heard a rumble of voices and the tramp of boots on the walk. Some men were coming up the incline, guns swinging from cartridge belts. Some of the Rafter A bunch, led by the toothless Cliff De-Long. The lips of DeLong's indented mouth were drawn so tight that the old man look of his fairly young face seemed more pronounced than usual. Two of the men with DeLong he recognized, Charlie Santo and the tense, red-bearded Eddie Toll.

If they saw Yale they gave no sign. He turned away, thankful he would soon see the last of this country. As he moved away from the shop he heard DeLong's gummy voice say, "Byerly, you sold some rifles to the hill bunch over at Aspen Springs."

"That I did," the gunsmith admitted.

"They're a bunch of outlaws, and you're not to deal with them no more," DeLong warned.

Yale halted, glancing over his shoulder. He saw Byerly's fat face turn red. "A man's got a right to run his business to suit himself!" Byerly cried. "The big outfits give me damn little business. Now clear out, DeLong, I'm busy."

"The hill bunch are rustlers. Nobody from this town gives 'em a hand. You understand?"

Yale felt a twitching along his jaws. He swung around and started back for the shop. He felt a hand snap to his arm. Turning, Yale had a fist half-raised when he saw it was Josh Wheatley.

"Keep out of it, Yale," the sheriff warned softly, and tried to draw him away.

Yale stood his ground. "Are you going to allow DeLong to bait Byerly?"

"This is not our affair." The pressure of his fingers increased on Yale's arm. For a moment Yale considered knocking the hand aside. But he allowed Wheatley to lead him to the opposite side of the street.

Belligerent voices continued to spill from the gunshop, and Yale said thinly, "This is one of the reasons I want to take Thela away from here."

"If you can pry her out of that house," Wheatley smiled. "I just heard of a business proposition that might interest you, Yale. You wouldn't have to leave here after all. Let's walk down to Quincy's and discuss it over a drink."

Yale only half heard him. He was staring across the street. Byerly's sheaf of pomaded hair had come loose from the bald dome to curl up like a wave of river water. DeLong stood with his back to the door, his shoulders rigid.

Yale said, "I wish I had the proof that DeLong is the one who shot me in the back."

"Proof on anybody at Rafter A is just something you don't get in this country. And what gave you the idea it was DeLong?"

When another yell burst from the gun shop, Yale said, "It just occurred to me that your job is to keep the peace in this town."

"To a point."

"Why don't you tell DeLong it's none of his business how Byerly sells his guns or to whom?"

His future father-in-law gave him a patient smile. "You haven't been here long, Yale. Not in terms of the old timers. The nesters over at the springs have given the big outfits hell from time to time."

"They never rustled a head of my beef."

"You aren't big enough, maybe. You see Byerly is intelligent. He's kind of theirs. He keeps the hill bunch stirred up. He tells 'em how to do things and—"

A sob of pain and anger burst from the shop. A crowd had drifted up, attracted by the loud voices. Cliff DeLong was holding Byerly by the front of his shirt.

Yale swore. "Josh, for God's sake, aren't you going to take a hand in this?"

"Take my advice and keep out of it."

Angered, Yale ignored Wheatley and started for the shop. He was in the center of the street when he saw Byerly twist free of DeLong's grasp and rush deeper into his shop. There he put a fat hand over a revolver on the work bench. Yale slowed. There was something in the way the Rafter A men had parted at Byerly's attempt to reach a weapon, that made him think this whole operation had been planned.

In the growing crowd Wheatley finally raised his voice. "DeLong, you'd better clear out now. Go down to Quincy's and cool off."

If the Rafter A foreman heard him above the din of shouting, running men, he gave no indication.

"Pick up that gun, Byerly," DeLong taunted, "if you're so bent on it!"

Byerly hesitated, perspiring. He stepped away from the work bench, hands wide of his body.

Deliberately Cliff DeLong turned his back. With a jangle of spur rowels he started purposefully for the door.

A warning boomed from Charlie Santo's bull throat. "Watch it, Cliff!"

In one fluid, deadly movement DeLong spun. His two guns came up, spitting orange-red flame through the balls of smoke. The impact of the bullets drove Byerly against the wall where he clung for a moment. Then his legs folded.

41

He fell, bleeding across the unswept floor littered with old wadding, shell casings, bits of lead.

Yale found his voice before the others in the stunned crowd. "Byerly didn't have a hand on a gun when DeLong turned his back."

Wheatley looked grim. "If he didn't, you damn well better keep it to yourself."

Josh Wheatley stalked into the gunshop, the crowd pouring in after him to stare at the body.

"Vultures," Yale muttered.

Sickened by what he had seen, he hurried to his horse. All the way back to 88 he kept reliving the scene in the gunshop.

And his estimation of himself lowered even more than his estimation of Josh Wheatley.

Bill Striker was just closing the corral gate with a loop of wire when Yale rode in. "Looks like you just swallowed a saw-toothed snake, boss," the foreman drawled.

Yale felt a faint resentment at the way Striker addressed him. "Forget the boss part of it. Cliff DeLong killed Byerly. Why?"

Yale recounted the scene in town.

"Byerly was kin to the Peters clan over at Aspen Springs," Striker said. "Duel always aimed to run Rafter A cows in this whole end of the range. But Duel figures to buy you out, and that's something. The cheaper he can buy, the more money he thinks he'll have when Mark dies."

"You mean he'll get my ranch one way or another. Either buy it or shoot me dead."

"I tell you this, Mr. Braden—"

"So it's *Mister* Braden now. Why isn't it Yale? We've been calling each other by our first names for months."

Striker rolled a cigarette. "You can see how it is, Mr. Braden. A man who won't fight for what is his—"

"Can't you understand? I've had enough fighting in my life?"

"I had four years of it in the Rebellion myself."

"I didn't know that, Bill."

"Mebbe you and me even shot at each other a few times." Striker put a match flame to his cigarette. "I figured the war was over. I needed to keep the job I had here with the Englishman, and you seemed like a steady man to work for, who knew what he was doing. So I forgot about you bein' on one side in the war and me on the other."

"I'm just tired of smelling blood, Bill."

42

"You'll smell it here, if you stay. Duel is the man for it."

"Even Mark has no use for Duel."

"Duel's a thief," Striker said. "He sold Rafter A cows at Paso Del Norte. Cows he had no business selling. I know that for a fact. That's how come Duel got throwed in that Mex prison."

"I never did know the details," Yale said.

"The buyer was a Mex general. Because the general had a fancy uniform he figured he didn't have to pay Duel for them cows. He was wrong. The general got shot in the stomach. And they tossed Duel in prison. And waited for Mark to ransom him out."

"Tell me about the Channas, Bill."

"They ran the sort of country here you'd have liked, Mr. Braden. The old man had a strong hand and he kept things under control. But he died and his son took over. Then the Ashforks come. Mark had the Channa girl's father hung to a tree."

"And his reason for this murder?"

"Mark thought Ron Channa was a cow thief. It was later that he figured Duel had been rustling Rafter A cows for years. It was Duel who was the thief, not Channa."

"A mistake that would be a little hard to correct."

"That's why Mark wouldn't ransom Duel outa that Mex prison. There ain't much to choose between them Ashfork brothers, but I reckon Mark is the best. And he's the one who's goin' to die."

"I don't think Mark is so holy. He wants to make amends for past mistakes—" He started to say "by marrying the Channa girl." But he caught himself just in time. It wasn't his right to discuss it and perhaps by gossip bring further problems to the girl.

That evening Yale, wearing black broadcloth, presented himself at the Wheatley house in Rincon. Thela had decided to forgive him. A note came that afternoon by rider: Darling, I'm having guests for dinner. Don't disappoint me.

When he arrived in Rincon they said Mark Ashfork was dying slowly. It was only a matter of time. Yale had no luck in trying to see the rancher at the Gadsen House.

At the appointed hour Yale was welcomed by Thela. The guests were the Southworths, Ardin and Elsie, of the Rincon Hardware. Southworth, a fat man who late in the day powdered his cheeks to hide a shine of beard, shook Yale's hand. His wife was small, demure, if you did not notice her sharp little eyes.

43

It was a satisfying dinner. Yale was not in a mood for it, but he did not want to incur Thela's displeasure two nights in a row by not attending. Thela made a picture with candlelight touching her dark hair. Yale thought of Lucinda Channa sitting at this table so many times in the past.

Southworth said, "I dropped in on Mark today. He says he's going to buy your ranch, Yale. But the state of his health—" Southworth lifted plump hands, let them fall to the table. "He does seem poorly. I told him I'd see you here tonight and pass along the word about your ranch."

"You've certainly had more luck seeing him than I have," Yale said.

Southworth shrugged. "I understand he and Duel have been heard arguing."

Elsie Southworth said, "We had a little excitement in town."

"Excitement?" Yale said.

"She means the shooting of Byerly," Southworth said. "Byerly always did have a nasty temper. He undoubtedly provoked DeLong into shooting him."

Yale put down his fork. "I don't think that was the case at all."

Southworth looked mildly surprised, and Josh Wheatley said, "I made an official report on the matter. Ardin, you were right in your version of what happened." Then, forcing a stiff smile, the sheriff said, "Yale, that gunsmith wasn't an easy man to get along with."

"Was that a reason to kill him?"

"Darling—" Thela's eyes pleaded across the candle lit table.

Wheatley said, "Of course I'm sorry he's dead."

"It was cold blooded murder," Yale cut in.

Southworth frowned. "Yale, we've lived here longer than you. Byerly is no loss."

"He was a human being. Doesn't that mean anything?"

Southworth's plump cheeks reddened. "I confess that I don't hold with Cliff DeLong. But then a ranch the size of Rafter A needs to have a gunman on the payroll."

Elsie Southworth said, "Speaking of Rafter A, I saw Duel on the street today. I declare he's handsomer than he was before the Mexicans imprisoned him." Turning, she gave Thela a sweet smile. "I'm surprised some woman hasn't married him before this."

Yale gave Thela a swift glance across the table to note her

44

reaction. But Thela acted as if she hadn't heard. She was discussing the servant problem with Ardin Southworth.

"The Camacho woman does her work, but she argues with me constantly."

As Thela went into detail, Southworth glanced at his watch. They had finished dinner and their brandy. "I understand Rafter A is paying off their extra roundup hands tonight, Josh. There may be a bit of wildness in the streets. Guess we'd better go."

"Well, they're young fellas mostly," the sheriff replied. "If there's trouble, don't worry I'll hear about it." He gave a small laugh to indicate the burdens of office. "Then I'll go down and straighten things out."

"When a man lies dead," Yale declared, "there's little you can do toward straightening things out."

Josh Wheatley drew on his cigar. "We're talking about two entirely different situations," he said stiffly.

"My idea of law enforcement is to prevent killings."

"When you've lived in these parts as long as I have, I'll feel you're entitled to express an opinion as to how this town should be policed."

Southworth nodded. "Josh is right, Yale. I don't care to be badgered by some drunken cowboys. That's the only reason I want to get home early. But so far as the rest of it is concerned the big outfits do their own policing. And a good job they do, I'd say."

Yale was about to open his mouth, but felt Thela's nails on his arm begging for silence. He said he'd walk downtown with the Southworths and get his horse. But Thela insisted he stroll with her in the courtyard. When her father had left with the guests, "to take a turn around town," Thela gave Yale an angry glance.

"You shouldn't hold it against father because Byerly got himself shot."

"Maybe I hold it against myself."

The moon was pushing through a layer of clouds. He watched her reflectively, thinking how beautiful she really was. Vitally alive. Her animation always touched him. He often wondered how a girl like Thela could be the daughter of Josh Wheatley.

She said, "You'd better quit talking as you did tonight. It'll get around."

"You mean Rafter A won't like it." He caught her hands, but she drew away. "Thela, I want to make a new life for us in California. Away from—" He wanted to say, Away

45

from your father. "—away from everything that could destroy our chances for happiness."

"You would deprive me of my home?"

"A woman's home is wherever her husband finds he can best provide for her."

She made a small gesture. "You're just upset over that Byerly thing."

"I've seen my number of dead. No, I don't turn cold in the stomach because Byerly was shot to pieces. It was the manner of his dying that galls me."

"You'd take the part of a—a bunch of nesters?" Taking his silence for resentment, she said, "I do so want our married life to be spent in this house. Father will live at the hotel. He's wanted to for a long time."

"I fail to see the importance of this house." He looked around at the shadowed walls. "It could be presentable, I suppose. But it's rundown—"

"Together we could build it into what it was," Thela said eagerly. "Build it into even more than it was when the Channas owned it."

CHAPTER NINE

Something in her voice caused him to look around. "Why have you never tried to be friends with Lucy Channa?"

"Are you on such familiar terms that you call her Lucy?" Thela snapped. "When we went to school together it was Lucinda."

"I believe you hate her."

Thela looked away and said quite calmly, "Darling, if you sell the ranch, just what do you intend doing to make a living for us?"

"There are many possibilities. California—"

"Father said he spoke to you about a proposition. But that Byerly thing—" She cleared her throat, her eyes shining as she leaned against him. "Honey, I happen to know that the Gadsen House is for sale. Ten thousand dollars would more than swing it. Carter doesn't know a thing about running a hotel."

"And neither do I, I'm afraid."

"You're prideful." Her voice was on edge. "There's nothing disgraceful in owning a hotel. With father so close to Rafter A there would be many opportunities here."

"You mean a man in the inner circle would stand to make some money," he said dryly.

"If you want to put it that way, yes."

"But when Mark dies, then what?"

"Duel will run things."

"Does your father have an understanding with Duel?"

"Yes."

He studied the top of her bent head for a moment. "I was surprised to learn that Duel once courted you."

Slowly she folded her hands. They were sitting on the bench. "There was never anything serious between us."

Despite the talk of old romance, of buying hotels, Yale found himself seething. It showed in his face. Thela was looking at him in surprise. He felt small and mean because he had stood in a crowd of other citizens of this county and watched a man shot down like a dog. The sheriff had made his report. Even a merchant such as Southworth took

47

it upon himself to condemn not the murderer but the victim.

And Yale wondered had he been wearing a gun what his reaction would have been. And how would it have ended? With Cliff DeLong stretched dead on the walk in front of the gunshop? Or Yale Braden dead.

Worriedly Thela searched his eyes, then pressed herself against him. "Darling, I want to marry you very much." As he reached for her she spun away, moving through a gate into a grove of dark trees. Over her shoulder she said, "You're in such a mood tonight, Yale."

She waited for his reply. Even though he could not see her face in the shadows, he sensed that she watched him closely to note his reaction. If he countered strongly, then she would change her tactics. He wondered then why he had never thought of her so objectively before. He remained silent, waiting.

"Father is rather silly, I suppose," she said. "To play the Rafter A game. But then he wants to see me married and happy. He likes you, Yale."

Yale realized she left him an opening to reluctantly admit he might have been partly at fault in his attitude toward her father. So he conceded, "Josh does have his problems, I suppose."

She put her arms about him and he looked across the top of her head to the uneven ridge of mountains crowding the night sky. A lonely, silent land. And he felt again that this country had become a part of him. Perhaps Thela was right. Maybe he should stay and give it a try and win his fight here.

She seemed to sense a change in him. "If you owned a hotel, you wouldn't be involved in range wars. You would not deal in cattle." Then she said abruptly, "Why do you love me, Yale?"

"For one thing, you nursed me when I was ill—"

"Don't tell me you fell in love with your nurse. I thought you loved me way before that."

"It's getting late, Thela. I really should get home—"

"I don't want you to go." Suddenly she sat upon the ground, her shoulders shaking. He could hear her sobbing. He put a hand to the back of her neck and rubbed gently on the warm flesh beneath the ringlets of dark hair.

"Don't cry," he said.

"But you want me to leave all this," she gasped. "You won't even give us a chance for happiness here."

Before he could say anything she reached up and caught his sleeve and pulled hard. For a moment he resisted. Then he sat down beside her. A small animal rustled in the undergrowth.

"Yale, you will stay for me, won't you?" she whispered. "Stay?"

"And fix this house and buy the hotel. And we will be very proper people."

"Does this house mean that much?"

"It's part of my life."

"I had some slight hope you would consider me of importance."

"In a few years, if you still want to, we can go to California." Her fingers dug into his arms. "Do this one thing and I—"

Instead of being touched by the way she pressed her mouth against his face he felt vaguely disturbed. Whatever proper words he sensed he should speak at this moment eluded him. Forcibly he tipped back her head and kissed her. Her arms flew about his neck.

He heard her whisper, "When I'm with you I'm completely shameless—"

Then she gave a small choking cry. And whatever gallant restraint that had held him in check began to crumble. Finally some last shred of fear seemed to stay her.

"No," she gasped. "No, Yale—not until we're married."

Somehow in his spinning mind the words had a hollow ring. He sat rigid for a moment, making no move toward her. Then she took his hands and placed them upon herself and whispered hoarsely, "Honey, I don't care. *I don't care!*"

A breeze came up, blowing coldly down from the higher elevations. And at last the violence of their embrace was touched by it and they broke apart. He sat up on the ground and mechanically brushed dirt from the knees of his trousers.

"It's all right, honey," she assured him. "It's all right. Don't feel shame. I don't. Now we can be married quickly."

As they neared the house he said, "You'd better fix your hair. The Camacho woman will think you've been in a high wind."

"Oh, I have, I have. In a very high wind, tumbling through all eternity with you. I never realized it could be like this."

He took her arm, wanting to feel a pride of possession. Somehow this female was a stranger. But he had committed

49

himself. And he was, he told himself, after all a gentleman of his word.

On the way home he tried to be objective. In some ways it was good to know that their emotions had reached the decision for them. Now there was no longer the hesitation, the doubt. He knew she loved him. And after all, her arguments about staying here, he supposed, did have some value.

With his older brother he had engaged in many enterprises in Missouri. If he put his mind to it, he could make a paying venture of the Gadsen House. Rincon was on the main route to the silver mines to the north. And there were more travelers and more freight being hauled each year. Gentlemen would welcome the convenience of a well-run hotel.

The matter was out of his hands now.

CHAPTER TEN

At midnight Yale was awakened by sounds of a wagon in the yard. Hastily dressing he went outside where Striker and some of his men were already gathered. It was a Rafter A wagon, driven by Pop Grimsby. Sharing the seat with him, nervously dry-washing bony hands, was the Reverend Burkhalter, who occasionally visited Rincon in a rather futile pursuit of soul saving.

Lying on a pile of blankets in the bed of the wagon was Mark Ashfork. Yale took a lantern from Striker, thrust it into the wagon bed. Mark's face was drawn and without color. His eyes seemed unusually large and fever bright.

Yale said, "I tried to see you today. The hotel clerk said you were sleeping—"

Mark Ashfork lifted a hand to shut him off. "Never mind that—" His voice faltered, then gained strength. "Hatcher says his niece was some taken with your arguments on my behalf."

"I gave no arguments on your behalf. I only told her—"

"Her uncle thinks different. Now listen to me. Your debt ain't discharged yet, Yale Braden."

"You said all I had to do was deliver your message."

It seemed to take most of Mark Ashfork's strength to violently shake his head. "You're comin' with us."

Yale leaned into the wagon. The smell of sickness brought to Yale a memory of red clay and dying men in a Virginia woods.

"Grimsby's the only man I can trust. Outside of you, Braden."

"You can't force the Channa girl to marry you."

"No force to it. She's half convinced I'm right."

"She'll never consent to be your wife."

"I aim to marry with her." For a moment Mark Ashfork's breathing was heavy. He had one hand pressed to the layers of bandage that covered his chest. "Then I can die in peace."

"You won't die in peace. You'll leave her a legacy of death."

"Enough of that. I don't have the strength to argue. Get

51

your horse and come with us. The Channa girl is on the fence. You could sway her to my side."

"I don't think so."

"Braden, I'm dying. Same as you were dying the day I packed you twenty miles to town. You're here tonight only because I saved you."

"I don't know. I just don't know—"

"I haven't much time, goddammit. If you got any decency you'll pay your debt like a man. Then I'll buy your ranch and to hell with it."

"How can I trust you to keep your word? You had Jake Byerly gunned down like a dog—"

"That was Duel's idea, not mine." Mark looked him in the eye. "My word on it, Braden. Twenty thousand in gold. You won't find another man in this country with nerve enough to buy your ranch. Now that Duel needs it for his Mex cows."

Yale climbed out of the wagon. Above him the forested peaks loomed velvet black, ominous. In the distance thunder growled at the night.

The Reverend Burkhalter, peering down from the seat, said, "We'd better get started. I think he's bleeding again."

*   *   *   *   *

The relatives were gathered in the Hatcher house, at this chill pre-dawn hour. Yale had helped carry Mark into the house and to a pallet on the floor. Martha Hatcher, in a faded dress, pulled out of shape by the body it covered, seemed fascinated by the sight of Ashfork holding his side, large yellow teeth clenched in pain.

"Fetch the girl," Ashfork groaned.

And finally Lucinda Channa came from the back part of the house, wearing a blue shirt, faded from the sun, canvas jeans and boots. Her yellow hair was knotted at the back of her neck. She did not look at Yale.

The Reverend Burkhalter seemed shocked by her appearance and made a point of asking her about it.

"I refuse to dignify this occasion," she said almost defiantly, "by dressing for it."

Pete Hatcher rubbed his hands together, grinning at Yale. "Looks like you didn't need to come after all. She's goin' through with it."

"She shouldn't be pressured," Yale said.

But Hatcher had turned away; his men, lined up across

the room, glared at Yale. Hatcher said, "Papers are all in order, Reverend. I tended to them myself."

"Get on with it," Mark Ashfork groaned from the pallet.

Yale held up his hand. "Just a minute, Miss Channa. Do you want to go through with this?"

Her blue eyes met his for the first time. He saw the full mouth tighten. "I suppose there are worse fates," she said quietly.

The ceremony was completed in a matter of minutes. Lucinda Channa refused to stoop and allow Mark Ashfork to slip the ring on her finger. This ritual she performed herself. When Mark Ashfork tried to grope for her hand she jerked away.

And when it was over he said heavily, glaring up at her from where he lay on the floor, "At least you could kiss your husband."

Turning, she walked into another room. And before the door closed on her Yale saw that she was tugging the ring from her finger.

When Mark Ashfork was carried back to the wagon, Yale said, "I've done my part. Now do yours."

But the long trip in the wagon seemed to have tired Ashfork. He lay with eyes closed, as if not hearing Yale.

"Braden, I wouldn't bother him about business," the reverend said. "It's been a strain on him."

The wagon pulled out for town, raising a cloud of dust. Yale frowned, thinking, If Mark can make a round trip in a jolting wagon, he must not be as damn bad hurt as he lets on. Or maybe not as bad hurt as he thinks he is.

CHAPTER ELEVEN

In the morning he went to the cookshack and took his accustomed place at the head of the table. Striker occupied the chair at the opposite end. The crew sat on benches. When Alex Beacham brought in the food they began to eat. Beacham was seldom without the pungent odor of whiskey on his breath. But he had never been too drunk to cook, and he had a certain talent for the preparation of food. So Yale said nothing about the numerous bottles that Beacham kept hidden about the ranch.

Some of the men were talking about the shooting of Byerly. Larry Arthur brushed aside a lock of pale hair and said heatedly, "It was damn murder, that's what it was."

"Byerly could fix a gun all right," another rider spoke up, "but he sure had a loud mouth."

Larry Arthur straightened on the bench. "Byerly was kin of mine."

Yale looked up from his plate of steak and beans. Silence was heavy. Yale said, "Byerly was related to the Peters clan up in the hills."

"So am I," Arthur stated. It was the first time Yale realized that one of the hill crowd worked for him. "I come from East Texas," Arthur went on to explain, "where we first landed after we quit Tennessee. Then I come over here. But I couldn't get along with Uncle Jer."

"I'm sorry Byerly was killed, Larry," Yale said.

"Thanks, Mr. Braden."

"Let's forget the *Mister* Braden part of it."

Larry Arthur flushed. "Bill Striker said we oughta show you some respect."

"Since when?" Yale demanded quietly.

Striker said, "I just thought you'd like it better that way."

"We've been calling each other by first names, Bill. Have I changed that much?"

Striker did not look up. He was giving two of the 88 men their orders. They were to ride the north ridge, which bordered Rafter A, to see if there were any signs of unusual activity on the part of the big neighbor.

54

"With Mark dead," Striker finished, "reckon Duel will start his move."

Yale said, "How do you know Mark is already dead?"

"It ain't likely for a man to live after a steer horn has busted into his lung."

Yale finished chewing a piece of fried steak. He laid aside his knife. "As you boys know I'm selling this ranch. To Mark Ashfork if he lives long enough. If not, then to someone else." He started to tell them that each man would receive a bonus. But he decided to let this come as a surprise.

Striker leaned back in his chair. "Duel made you an offer for this place. That's where it'll end, Mr. Braden. You won't have no other buyers. That is if Mark don't pay you."

"You mean I'd personally have to fight Duel, if I planned to sell somewhere else?"

"Reckon that's about the way it is, Mr. Braden."

Yale cleared his throat. "I'm not leaving New Mexico as I intended. I— If possible, I'm going to buy the Gadsen House."

Striker looked incredulous. "A ho-tel?"

"I know it seems a little odd, but my future wife—" Yale could feel heat in his cheeks, realizing how it must sound; that Thela already was breaking him to harness. Under the scrutiny of his men he experienced embarrassment and also a rising anger. "There's one thing I want you to bear in mind. None of you are to get yourselves shot up because of this ranch. If there's trouble, I want you to stay out of it."

"What if Duel tries to move them Mex cows on our range?" Striker said.

"Let's hope he doesn't try."

"You don't know Duel."

Yale felt he should make amends for his short temper of a moment ago. "I've grown to like you boys. I don't want to see any of you die because of me." For an awkward instant he felt trapped by sentiment, so he added crisply, "I hope we understand each other."

He trudged up the path to the house. In what had once been a spare bedroom he had made a sort of office. He sank into a swivel chair before a spur-marked desk and stared at the walls lined with his books. He considered opening a certain drawer and taking a drink from a bottle kept for medicinal purposes and for the alleviation of periods of depression such as this. He glanced idly at the lamp, seeing it was low in coal-oil. And he thought irritably, Why hadn't

Beacham tended to it? These minor irritations lately were putting him out of sorts. He wondered what had gotten into him.

Then he thought of Thela, and last night. And he was surprised, when he analyzed his reactions, how objective he could be. A memory that seemed unclouded by intense emotion. And for some reason he found himself weighing her against the defiant Lucinda Channa who had consented to marry a dying man.

He thought of the Gadsen House in Rincon, with its draughty halls and the banging of doors, the odors of the many occupants and the things they did behind those doors. And he suddenly felt cramped, as if shut off from this world of open air and mountains he could see through the window.

He looked around, idly wondering how Thela would fit into a house like this. But would he himself be satisfied to stay here the rest of his life? Was the cattle business in New Mexico all he had thought it would be? And yet, when he looked around, he felt a tug of emotion when he thought of the plans he'd had when he first came here. But then he supposed the Gadsen House would offer as much future as any he had planned for himself. Nothing worked out quite as we hoped, was the thought that darted through his mind.

Even marriage with Thela would not provide quite the smooth path he had once envisioned.

The sound of riders cutting through the aspens from the east alerted him.

Yale stepped to the yard, remembering he had forgotten his hat. In this country a bareheaded man was not considered dressed when he was out of doors. The hell with it, he thought. At least the operator of a hotel was not expected to observe such a custom. He could do as he well pleased, and the fact that he carried no long-barreled pistol would not be looked upon as such a breach of custom as it was now when he ranched for a living.

Jeremiah Peters, bony legs hugging the barrel of a dun, came up with six of his men. The faces of the riders were stony. They all had the scrawny, loose-muscled build of the woodsman.

Old man Peters drew reins, to stare down at Yale over his jutting white beard. His boots were as wrinkled as his face.

"Step down," Yale invited, as the old man glared.

Peters ignored the suggestion. "I ain't ever had much truck

with you, Braden, 'cause you fought Nawth in the war. But since you come here you minded your own business. And you took this place that never was worth much when that Englishman had it, and you made something out of it. And I've admired you for it."

"Thanks for the kind words."

"The kinds words is finished," the old man grunted. "I s'pose you know if you sell to Rafter A it'll put 'em right up against our line. We don't like it. They'll be crowdin' us too much. Eighty-Eight was a buffer between us, but now—"

Yale considered his position. "If Mark doesn't live to buy I'll shade my price and give you a chance at it."

"Us Peters never had no money. All we got is guns and wimmen folks and kids and cows and whisky to drink. That was all I was ever taught a man needed. That and his self-respect."

"It's a good philosophy," Yale agreed.

"When you was shot that time we felt almighty bad. We worried that mebbe you'd think one of us done it."

"It did cross my mind. But then I decided you'd have no reason. Unless it was a holdover from the war."

"We lost the war and we hated to lose it. And we don't feel rightly toward them that whupped us. But it ain't our way to shoot a man in the back."

"I have recently come to a conclusion about who shot me. And who ordered it done."

Jeremiah Peters rubbed at his mustache. "I wish to hell it was Duel Ashfork dyin' instead of Mark. Mark give us all trouble when he first come here. But when Mark makes a mistake, he admits up to it. That's more'n Duel would do."

"You're talking about the death of Ron Channa?"

"Mark never should've had Ron hung, and killed them other Channa boys. It was Duel stole them cows, not Channa."

"So I've heard."

Yale saw Peters stiffen in the saddle when some of the 88 men drifted up. The old man was glaring at Larry Arthur who stood, hands on hips, a lock of straw-colored hair curved below the band of a sweated hat.

"Hello, Uncle Jer," Arthur said.

"Why don't you come home where you belong?"

"I'm doin' rightly well here." Larry Arthur nodded to the youngest of the riders with Jeremiah Peters, a lank man with a prominent Adam's apple. "Hello, Eph."

57

Eph said, "We miss you, Larry. Damn if we don't."

Jer Peters had turned from Larry Arthur and was shaking his finger at Yale. "We've had bad times since the war. I've had some of my boys shot up. And there's one that went back to Tennessee who won't never be able to use his legs again. The Rafter A crowd beat him up. And it was Duel who shouted 'em on."

"We've all had some rough times," Yale put in.

The old man lost some of his truculence. "I'd be obliged if you'd hang on here, Braden. Long as you've done it this long. It would make things easier all around."

"I have my own plans—"

"All right then, I tell you my warnin'." The old man's mouth tightened. "You sell to Rafter A, consider yourself without friends in the hills."

"Aren't you being a little unreasonable?"

Peters leaned over the horn. "I hear how Byerly got killed. And I hear you was there when it happened. I aim before I die to kill Cliff DeLong for that cowardly murder. Maybe then it'll shame them who stood by and watched a man blown to pieces."

Peters drove in the spurs, cut across the pasture and up through the aspens with his men splashing through the creek in his wake.

Bill Striker said thoughtfully, "Before Duel got mixed up in that Mex prison he claimed Peters and his bunch rustled Rafter A cows. Now that he's back he'll likely whistle the same old tune again."

"Peters looks like a man who can take care of himself," Yale offered.

"It's Wheatley's job, but now that you're marrying his daughter—Well, I reckon you wouldn't expect the sheriff to do anything about it."

"Bill, if you don't mind, leave my coming marriage out of this. I don't approve of Wheatley. But he's Thela's father. Let's leave it at that."

Color stained Striker's cheeks. "How the hell did your side ever manage to win the war?"

"You imply that I'm gutless!" And Striker just looked at him, then started away. Yale called him back. "Whatever happens between the Peters crowd and Rafter A is none of our business. I don't want a man on my payroll to risk his neck for this ranch."

"So you already said."

"I'm selling out—one way or another. I want no part of this."

Yale went into the house, slamming the door behind him. He hadn't wanted to blow off like that at Striker. But damn it, he was getting tired of these insinuations that he was afraid to fight.

After the noon meal Yale rode to town to try and conclude his deal with Mark Ashfork. At the hotel he was surprised to learn that Mark had been taken by wagon out to Rafter A.

"Then he must be some improved," Yale said to the hotel clerk who had given him the information.

"Considerable." The clerk cleared his throat. "If you buy the hotel I hope I can stay on here—"

But Yale hardly heard him. On the veranda he watched the wind tear clouds to shreds against the higher peaks. He was vaguely troubled when he thought of Lucinda Channa in light of the fact that her husband seemed to be taking a long time to die. And after what the clerk had told him he couldn't see Mark Ashfork unless he rode out to Rafter A. And that was a considerable piece of riding at this time of day. For a moment he considered the idea, then discarded it.

In Quincy's he had a drink and listened to the talk. The handful of drinkers at the bar stayed by themselves.

When he stepped onto Mesilla Street, he noted the way people looked at him. And he realized that although he had never been considered one of them, he now noted outright antagonism on some faces. And he knew the word was out that he would not make a stand against his enemies, in the only way these people could comprehend—with a gun.

Clenching his fists, he started away from the saloon.

A voice reached him: "Carpetbagger bastard!"

Halting, Yale looked around to identify the speaker. In his wish to avoid violence there was no part of the code that said he couldn't use his fists. He saw a knot of men standing down the walk.

One of them, Charlie Santo, stepped away from the others, his barn-wide body throwing a blocky shadow across the walk. He cuffed back his hat on his shaved skull.

"Want me to say it louder, Braden?"

"I didn't care for your reference to me." In these post war years any man who had worn blue could be classed as a carpetbagger by his former enemies. There was scarcely a lower name that could be applied to a man.

Santo stepped forward, the walk shaking under his weight.

59

A mantle of tension settled over the street. People were looking around, some grinning, some frozen.

A man said hoarsely, "Don't Braden know he'll lose his brains if he tangles with a man Santo's size?"

Down the block a frightened woman gathered up two children and hustled them across the street. She kept looking back over her shoulder at the towering Rafter A rider and the slender owner of 88.

Coming to a halt, Santo laughed. "Want me to say it again, Braden?"

"Never mind," Yale grunted. He started to turn, but Santo put out a hand and got him by a shoulder. The strong fingers bit into his flesh like steel clamps.

A thrust of rage burst through Yale's decision to let the matter with Santo drop; that no purpose could be served in trying to fight against such overwhelming odds. He spun, glaring up at Santo's wide face. Knowing he was a fool to let anger shatter his resolve.

"I've had just about enough!" he cried. He came to his toes and struck at Santo's heavy jaw.

Obviously not expecting Yale's quick reaction, Santo gave a grunt. He fell back, blinking his eyes. But he quickly recovered. Shouting obscenities he lunged forward.

Yale caught him with a savage blow to the pit of the stomach, danced away. Santo lashed out, knuckles just missing the side of Yale's face. Men, yelling, poured from the saloon to watch the battle.

Yale circled, feeling the strength going out of his legs. And he felt a stab of pain at the newly-healed wound under his armpit.

Again Santo charged. In stepping back to avoid the powerful rush, Yale caught his bootheel in a crack in the plank walk. He fell heavily, shaking dust from the planks.

As Santo aimed a kick at his head Josh Wheatley's voice angled in. "Santo, that's enough!" the sheriff ordered.

But Santo came on and Wheatley stepped in close. "Charlie, I said that's enough."

Santo drew up and looked around at Wheatley's cocked revolver.

Yale got to his feet, picked up his hat. "Thanks, Josh. I guess I owe you something for that."

Wheatley holstered his gun. He came over and put a hand on Yale's shoulder. "You ought to know better. You're too soon out of bed to fist fight a man of Santo's size." The sheriff was trying to lessen the tension with a grin.

"Next time bring Striker and your whole crew. Maybe—just maybe—all of you might be able to handle Santo."

Yale looked around. The big Rafter A segundo had gone into Quincy's. The crowd was breaking up. He nodded to Josh Wheatley and limped down to get his horse.

CHAPTER TWELVE

When Yale arrived from Rincon, he saw a strange team and wagon in the yard. Ownership of the outfit was not long in doubt, for as he neared the house he saw Pete Hatcher's scrawny frame propped against the porch rail. Martha Hatcher overflowed a chair on the porch. Yale's spirits lifted when he saw Lucinda Channa, her yellow hair touched by sunlight, pacing the yard.

Yale rode down, removing his hat to the ladies. The girl looked pale and drawn, but determined. She gave Yale a spare nod as he said, "This is a pleasant surprise, Miss Channa."

But Hatcher grunted the reason for the girl's tension. Mark Ashfork had sent for his wife. And she refused to go.

"You seem to have some influence with her, Braden," Hatcher explained, "so I took a chance and brung her over—"

"I'm afraid you're mistaken about influence," Yale snapped.

"She thinks you're pretty smart 'cause you read books—"

"Your niece seems to be the point of discussion, not my books." Yale started toward Lucinda, who stood near the tied team. She was a tall girl in faded shirt and jeans and worn boots. A portmanteau, probably containing her belongings, was lashed to the tailgate.

Hatcher swung around and blocked Yale. "You're the one helped show her the light about marryin' with Mark in the first place, Braden. Now you got to show her that it's a wife's place to be with her husband."

Yale stared at the narrow, unshaven face. "You've already sold her for Mark Ashfork's money. Why don't you let her make up her own mind?"

From the porch, Martha Hatcher said shrilly, "It's her duty."

"I'm a little surprised at you, Mrs. Hatcher," Yale said coldly.

Lucinda, her back straight, came up. "I told you Braden would have this reaction. So you wasted your time dragging me here, Uncle Pete."

"That's no way to talk." Her aunt was coming down the steps, perspiring in the spring heat.

"I intend leaving this country," Lucinda stated. "I will not go to that man. I married him only because you and Uncle Pete tried to make me believe it was my duty not to miss what you called opportunity."

Pete Hatcher's eyes were mean. "Damn it you got a husband and you go to him or I'll—" He tried to reach Lucinda, but she stood her ground. Yale shouldered her uncle aside.

"Enough of this," Yale ordered.

But Hatcher spun out of Yale's grasp and darted for the wagon. He had one hand on a rifle lying on the floorboards when Yale caught him. He swung Hatcher against a wagon wheel, tore the rifle free and unloaded it. He threw the shells across the yard.

Martha Hatcher rushed to her husband. "Pete, did he hurt you?"

Hatcher was glaring at Yale. "You better make Lucy come to her senses. I mean that."

Lucinda Channa made an angry gesture. "Uncle Pete, I will not go to Mark Ashfork. And that is final!"

With an oath Hatcher started for her again. Then, seeing Yale's hard face, he drew up. But he did say, "Lucy, either you take your rightful place with your husband. Or you ain't welcome no more at our house!"

Before the girl could reply, Yale snapped, "She's welcome to stay here." And when she looked at him in narrowed surprise, he added, "I'll take my blankets to the bunkhouse."

She lifted her chin. "I can't accept your hospitality."

"You have no choice Miss Channa. Do it for me. I feel partly responsible for getting you into this fix."

"But I just can't stay here!"

"If Mark Ashfork is hurt as bad as he says, he won't live anyway. I've seen too many men with a punctured lung. It's only a matter of days, perhaps, instead of hours. Wait here until it's over."

Hatcher's face was red with anger. "Mark won't like what you done, one damn bit."

"I don't give much of a hang whether he likes it or not. I'm getting all-fired fed up with certain elements in this country."

Despite Hatcher's threats, Yale untied the girl's portmanteau and carried it to the house. When he returned Martha Hatcher was clambering into the wagon.

63

"You're welcome to stay with your niece, Mrs. Hatcher, until a decision is reached—"

But Pete Hatcher, muttering under his breath, was already driving the wagon out of the yard. Dust lifted against the aspens.

"He'll probably go to Mark right off," Yale said.

The girl bit her lip. "I had my things packed. I intended going to the way station at Half Pine and getting the Mesilla stage. But they insisted I come here. To avoid argument I did as they asked."

"They're a greedy pair."

"I know." She gave Yale a small sad smile, adding quite candidly, "I sensed you would take my part."

"You get some rest."

At supper Yale carried a tray up to the house.

She seemed worried. "I've been thinking—"

"Forget what people will say."

"If I stay under your roof even for one night. It will turn Mark Ashfork against you."

"I tell you, if Mark has a punctured lung, he won't live. And besides, Mark isn't the first enemy I've faced."

"But Rafter A— It could swallow you up." She stared out the window where a deep velvet twilight spread across the yard. "A friend of my mother's lives in Mesilla. She said I was welcome to visit any time."

He gestured at the tray he had placed on the table. "Eat and then get a good night's sleep. I'll see that you get to Mesilla at the proper time."

She gave him a warm smile. "Thela is fortunate to have a strong man at her side in these troubled times."

"I'm not so strong. I have many weaknesses."

"We all do. My grandfather was the last strong one in our family."

"Good night, Miss Channa," he said, and the thought came to him then with startling force, that she was really Mrs. Mark Ashfork.

"Call me Lucy."

"Wouldn't you prefer Lucinda?"

She shook her head. "It reminds me of the things we once had."

Yale stared at her a minute, then said, "You and Thela have known each other a long time?"

"She lived with us when she was a little girl. Her father broke horses for us."

64

Yale was surprised. "I can't imagine Josh Wheatley in that role."

"He's smart. He didn't stay long as horsebreaker." Lucy lifted the towel that covered the tray of food. "I carried on so, my father sent Thela to school with me in St. Louis. By the time we returned here her father was sheriff."

"Then you did a lot for Thela when she was a girl."

"She was my friend. I wanted her to share, that's all."

"You had so much and Thela so little. Horsebreaker." Yale shook his head. "I don't imagine she cared for that."

"I always liked Thela. But now—well, we've grown apart."

When he returned to take the evening meal at the cookshack, his men were talking in low tones. He sensed an air of tension.

"Larry Arthur hasn't come back," Striker said.

Yale was so preoccupied with Lucy Channa's troubles, that it took him a moment for the news to reach his consciousness. Striker seemed concerned because the rider hadn't arrived back for supper.

"Maybe you worry too much, Bill," Yale said.

"It's the times that makes a man worry, Mr. Braden."

Yale spent a restless night. Not since the war had he slept with so many men about him. They snored and scratched themselves and muttered in their sleep.

When Beacham stuck his head in the doorway to announce breakfast, Larry Arthur still had not returned. And the opinion of some of the men that Arthur had spent the night in an 88 line shack, seemed a little thin now in the cold dawn.

After telling Beacham to take a tray to Miss Channa, Yale rode into the Mogollons, in the direction Larry Arthur had taken yesterday when he left to scout the mountains.

Before he crossed the creek Bill Striker swung in beside him. "I'll go with you," the foreman announced.

When they paused later to to let their horses blow, Yale said, "Bill, a man nearly dies and then he really learns to appreciate life."

"Reckon so, Mr. Braden."

"For kee-rist sake, will you quit calling me Mr. Braden? Do you think because I don't want to see my men hurt that I'm a coward?"

"That hoss of yours was shot. It could've been a man. You never got mad enough to do anything about it."

"I did get mad. Damn it, Bill—"

They started riding again. "I got one bit of advice, Mr.

Braden. I'd start diggin' around in the bottom of my trunk for a belt gun."

"I gave my revolver away before I came here. I have no intention of purchasing another."

"Then if I was you I'd marry Thela Wheatley damn sudden and take her to California like I planned." Striker spat over the horn. "Maybe there are some men who can get out of trouble by just talkin' about it. But I never met any."

Striker broke off. They had both seen it at the same time. The 88 sorrel, still saddled, its reins hung up in a thicket of shin oak.

Yale spurred forward, feeling a tautness in his chest. "Is this the horse Arthur rode yesterday?"

Striker grimly nodded. He had pulled his rifle from its scabbard and was peering around in the trees.

Yale looked the animal over, feeling a slight relief. There was no blood on the saddle. "Apparently he was thrown."

"Not Larry Arthur," Striker stated positively. "There ain't a hoss on Eighty-Eight can throw that boy."

Striker pulled the sorrel's tangled reins free of the shin oak. With Striker leading the sorrel, they back-tracked the animal up the steep trail.

Some miles east they came within sight of the 88 line shack. And then Yale saw the four stakes driven into the ground in front of the shack. The man spread-eagled between them was Larry Arthur.

All he wore was his pants. The thongs that held wrists and ankles to the stakes had cut so deeply that the flesh was puffed and discolored.

Yale felt a cold twitching along his nerves as he swung down. At first he thought Arthur was dead. Then he saw the faint stirring of the chest under the mat of flies. Even before he brushed them aside he noted that the chest hair had been singed, the flesh beneath it seared by a hot iron that had imprinted upon him the Ashfork brand, Rafter A.

Stunned, Yale shifted his gaze to a word scratched into the soft ground above Arthur's head: COWTHIEF.

Beyond, lay a dead cow with a crudely reworked brand. A running iron had been thrust into the cold ashes of a dead fire. Someone had done an obviously clumsy job in trying to change a Rafter A to Yale's 88.

"Get some water!" Yale snapped at Striker, and again brushed at the cluster of flies.

While Striker untied a canteen from his saddlehorn, Yale used his pearl-handled pocket knife to cut through the

66

leather thongs. The 88 rider's eyes opened and for a moment he stared blankly. Then his gaze focused on Yale.

"Was beginnin' to think you fellas would never get here," he whispered. "I hung on, but—"

"Take it easy," Yale cautioned, and bent low over the injured man's lips. "Who did it? Was it Duel?"

"Cliff DeLong," Arthur managed to get out after several tries. "It was late yesterday. I was on my way back when they catched me."

Striker lumbered up with water in a canteen. Yale took it and carefully lifted Arthur's head. The man managed to swallow a few drops.

Larry Arthur's brow was hot with fever. The flies had done their ugly work at the burn on his chest. He was trying to speak again.

"DeLong said I worked over their brand on a Rafter A cow—" Suddenly Arthur's young face with its stubble of pale beard, went slack. A fly descended on one of the staring eyes.

Striker capped his canteen, his lips white. "I've seen 'Paches work. But this is worse than them." His voice was shaking. "This is one white man to another."

Yale stood up. "You take Larry's body back to the ranch." Yale caught up his horse and mounted.

"Where you goin', Mr. Braden?"

"To see the sheriff about this."

"Yeah," Striker said sourly. "I figured that's about what you'd do."

Yale looked around at his foreman as he reined in his horse. The scent of blood was making it hard to handle. "Bill, I want you and the men to stay out of this. That's an order."

"This ain't the Union Army you're talkin' to, Mr. Braden. We got our own way of handlin' things without orders from you."

"The man who follows me is fired!"

For an answer Striker turned his back and brought up Arthur's sorrel and prepared to lash on the body. Yale knew a further exchange with Striker would only widen the chasm between them. He rode off, pushing his horse.

By the time Yale reached town it was twilight.

CHAPTER THIRTEEN

A few loafers in front of the livery broke off their discussions of how the South lost the war, what was the matter with women these days, and why a man with two thousand head of beef had no range unless he hastened the death of his own brother and appropriated, by one means or another, Rafter A.

They turned to stare at Yale Braden, who spurred in from the alley onto Mesilla Street.

" 'Pears that somebody built a fire under that Yankee man," said one.

Yale's first hunch concerning the whereabouts of the sheriff was right. He found Wheatley bellied up to the bar in Quincy's, regaling the hangers on with a story of early Rincon. Two reps from the big outfits south of Rincon were among the listeners.

Yale, giving the men a curt nod, drew Wheatley aside. The sheriff's mouth under the bristly mustache showed displeasure.

"What's the hurry, Yale? I was just telling the boys about the time I—"

"Josh, I lost a good man today. Larry Arthur was branded on the chest with a Rafter A iron."

Wheatley went white. "You sure?"

"Cliff DeLong killed him. I want to swear out a warrant."

Wheatley bit his lip. "I wouldn't go off half-cocked like this, Yale—"

"I had a feeling this would be your reaction," Yale said coldly.

"Now, just a minute—"

"But I wanted to hear you say it with my own ears so there'd be no mistake." Turning his back, Yale started for the door.

Wheatley hurried to catch up with him. "Get a cinch on your temper, Yale. Some of the Rafter A boys are in town—" And when Yale just kept walking, the sheriff said hoarsely, "Don't be a damn fool. You could ruin everything for yourself and Thela—"

At the door Yale said, "Josh, have you finished your speech?"

The buzz of talk in the saloon had quieted.

"Look, Yale, you have no proof it was Rafter A—"

"Proof is the brand on Arthur's chest. He lived long enough to tell me about it."

Yale walked out, letting the doors slap at Wheatley's face. He rode up the hill and around the corner, climbing again. He dismounted in front of Byerly's gun shop.

A bulky man smoking a cigar was sweeping out.

Yale said, "Are you taking over here?"

"Sheriff said for me to keep the place open. Some of the boys had guns being fixed here and—"

"I want a revolver. I'll pay for it later. I'm Braden of the Eighty-Eight."

"I know you, Braden. Fixin' to marry with Wheatley's daughter. Reckon anything you want is all right.

Yale followed him to a cabinet. The man opened a drawer containing a collection of revolvers.

Yale studied them a moment. "Do you happen to know if Byerly had a personal gun?"

"Yeah." The man picked out a .44 with a "B" burned into the grips. He handed it over.

Yale checked the loads, drew back the hammer several times and let it down to test the action. He shoved the weapon in his waistband, and buttoned his coat over it.

"I'm looking for Cliff DeLong. Have you seen him?"

"Fella told me DeLong's hoss is tied in front of Maude Telfer's place. Was there about an hour ago."

Clouds had swung in from the north and Yale felt the first warm splatter of rain against his face as he rode into Muldoon Alley. The establishment run by Maude Telfer was set back in a grove of cottonwoods behind a weed-grown lot. On Saturday nights the long, low 'dobe building seemed lively enough. But now only two horses were at the rail. Yale noted that both mounts wore Rafter A brands.

Looping reins over the chewed hitch rack he took a moment to get himself under control. He wanted no rage to hamper the efficiency of his reflexes. But the picture of Larry Arthur's tortured face would not fade from his mind. He glanced at the windows and could see no movement.

Drawing a deep breath he ducked under the rail. The front door was unlocked. He stepped in to a small deserted barroom with three tables, some chairs and a long bench. A sort of waiting room, he supposed. A man's hat lay on the bar beside a bottle of whisky.

He loudly cleared his throat and in a moment a heavily-built woman padded from the rear, fussing with a loose knot of flaming red hair. A beefy neck was minimized, at least partially, by bright beads looped about her throat. For a moment she stared blankly.

"Ah, Mr. Braden," she said, recognizing him. "It's the first time you've honored us with a visit." She gestured at the bar. "A drink first?"

"I'm looking for Cliff DeLong."

The eyes grew wary. "I think you've come to the wrong place."

"I have an important message for him. It concerns Rafter A."

Her eyes, a lemon color, took on a new sharpness. "I don't want trouble here."

Purposely he spread his hands away from his body. Her gaze quickly settled at his buttoned coat.

"Oh, yes, I remember," she murmured, obviously relieved. "You're the one who never wears a gun. All right, I'll see if Cliff can be disturbed. But I warn you, he may resent—"

"It's important that I speak to him. He'll understand."

She hesitated, then walked away, her backside bulging hugely at each step along the corridor. He heard a door open, a murmur of voices.

Tensely he looked around, smelling cheap perfume, stale whisky. So different from the Saturday nights of shouting and laughter he'd heard from a distance.

A girl deep in the building protested. "Cliff, don't go. Let him wait."

And Cliff DeLong. "Be right back, Angie. Come along, Charlie. Let's see what the blue-belly wants."

Then DeLong appeared in the corridor, hatless, needing a shave. His black shirt was powdered with dust. His shaggy hair needed cutting. A whisky flush had settled over his indented face. But his eyes seemed clear enough. He came to stand a few feet away.

"What message you got for Rafter A, Braden?"

Then Yale saw Charlie Santo amble in and lean his bulk against the wall. The segundo was grinning. On one side of the jaw was a slight discoloration. Yale hoped it was from his fist, when they'd briefly tangled on the street ... Santo's hook-

70

ing of the fingers of his right hand in the belt above a bone-handled revolver was almost insolent.

Deliberately Yale made his features expressionless as he followed an old and familiar pattern.

"One of my men was found this morning, DeLong. With a Rafter A branded on his chest."

"I'll be damned," DeLong said with a faint grin. "How about that, Charlie?"

Santo only laughed and Yale said, "Larry Arthur was treated badly."

"Ain't the first man in these parts to be so treated," DeLong stated. Evidently he had been roused from a pleasant interlude. But he had not neglected to belt on his two guns.

"Must've been some of the hill crowd used our brand on him," Santo put in.

"Come to think of it," DeLong said, "we missed an iron a couple weeks ago. Them thieves likely stole it."

"You know that's a lie," Yale said quietly.

"Braden, why don't you get the hell out of here?" DeLong said.

"I'm pretty certain you shot me in the back last year."

"Them nesters shot you."

"Just before he died, Larry Arthur named his assailant. You can't crawl out of it this time."

"Assailants now," DeLong mocked. "Ain't we fancy."

"Arthur said you're the one who did it, DeLong."

DeLong laughed shortly, showing the receded gums. "If Arthur's dead, he sure as hell can't tell it again, now can he?"

"No, he can't. But I wasn't the only witness to what he said."

The harshness of Yale's voice caused DeLong to stare at the tail of Yale Braden's coat, as if to search for the snout of a holstered revolver. Then, satisfied, he lifted his gaze to Yale. "You better run, blue-belly. While you still got legs."

Yale said, "You don't have the guts to move against the big outfits. So you move against the little ones."

"We'll get you first, Braden. Then we'll take the hill crowd. We'll run cows forty miles into the Mogollons now that Duel's back."

"That's irresponsible talk and you know it."

There was a step in the corridor and Santo said, "Here comes Eddie. He's just in time for the fun."

DeLong, noticing the surprise on Yale's face, burst out

71

laughing. "Eddie left his hoss with the smithy to get shod. That's how come there wasn't three hosses out front."

The redbearded Eddie Toll wore no hat. He was in his stocking feet. When he halted at the end of the bar, he sniffed the air. "Cliff, I smell Yankee polecat."

"Braden says they found one of their men with a Rafter A on his hide. You s'pose it could've been that cow thief we catched out?"

"The one that changed Rafter A into Eighty-Eight?" Toll drawled.

"Damn clumsy job of it he done," DeLong said.

Yale considered his position. Even though Toll had neglected to put on his boots he wore his gun. While Yale talked, he had been shifting around so that his back was to the front wall. Two men could be handled. But the addition of a third party made the odds overwhelming. In his anxiety to settle this he had not made certain how many men De-Long had with him. Well, he was committed now. One way or the other they'd kill him when they decided to quit having their fun and get it over with.

One thing for sure, in dealing with men such as these anything was fair. He remembered how DeLong had shot Byerly, with the man not even touching a weapon. And he would never forget the odor of burned flesh when he found Larry Arthur spread-eagled near a dead cow and a running iron. The rider keeping himself alive just long enough to tell who had done it. To be certain that no blame was put on the hill crowd. And this Charlie Santo and Eddie Toll had been part of it, along with the Rafter A foreman. Little doubt of that. They had finished their business, then decided to relax here at Maude Telfer's.

Yale held out his left hand toward Santo, nearly touching him. "What would you do if one of your men was branded like a steer?"

Santo laughed. "I dunno now, just what I'd do. Seein' as how I ain't a yellow-gutted Missouri bastard like you."

Cliff DeLong reached around for the bottle on the bar. Without taking his eyes from Yale he pulled the cork with his teeth and spat it on the floor. He took a long drink.

"Boys, I think we oughta tromp this snake—"

In that moment Yale's right hand went beneath his coat. The gun came swiftly out. He struck savagely to his left, the long steel barrel smashing Santo diagonally across the face. Santo dropped soundlessly. As Eddie Toll dug for his gun Yale's first shot caught him in the side. Toll spun against the bar with such force he lost his grip on the gun.

Caught by surprise, DeLong hurled the whisky bottle at Yale. It whipped across the top of his shoulder, crashing into the window behind him. So swiftly did DeLong drag up his guns that he began firing before Yale could even swing his weapon to cover the foreman.

In that frozen moment Yale braced himself for the impact. But DeLong hurried his shots. One cut through the already broken window. The other screamed in a ricochet against 'dobe bricks and buried itself in the ceiling.

DeLong never had a second chance. Yale tripped the hammer of the weapon that had belonged to Jake Byerly. The heavy caliber slug ripped into the widest part of DeLong's body. The foreman's knees caved. Desperately he tried to lift his guns. Yale fired again. DeLong's strangled cry of pain and rage was abruptly cut off. The right side of his throat was gone.

Yale felt the sting of powder in his nostrils. A movement caused him to lift his gaze from the men on the floor. The Telfer woman and one of her girls, a white-faced brunette, had crowded into the hall. They stared at Santo, who sat dazedly, bleeding into the hands pressed against his slashed face. Eddie Toll moaned, the right side of his shirt stained brown.

When he tried to stoop for his gun, Yale said, "Don't!"

Toll looked around, a hand pressed to his side.

DeLong lay on his side. A spot of color at the lips drawn tightly back against gums that had been so long without teeth.

As hysteria started to crumple the faces of the two women, Yale gathered up the guns. Neither Santo nor Toll made any attempt to stop him. Outside he threw the weapons into the cottonwoods. Then he rode out. When he reached Mesilla Street the Telfer woman found her voice and began to bellow. Men had already swarmed out of buildings.

At the edge of town Yale looked back. The street, thick in shadow, was nearly deserted as the crowd streamed toward Muldoon Alley.

As Yale started along the road, he noticed a dark body of riders pushing up through a stand of junipers. Alerted, he swung his horse toward the stable fence.

A familiar voice called, "Mr. Braden!"

It was Striker. The 88 foreman spurred up, the rest of the crew behind him. "We heard shots," Striker said, searching Yale's face in the twilight. "Was there trouble in town?"

"I told you to keep out of it. Damn it all—" Now reaction was setting in.

"We didn't aim to keep out of it," Striker said quietly. "What happened?"

"We'd better get out, in case there are more Rafter A men in town."

Striker cocked his head at the distant sounds of excitement coming from Mludoon Alley. But Yale was already moving in the direction of 88. Striker caught up with him, the others stringing along behind at a jog. There was a discussion in low tones, and Yale knew the men were talking about him. He had not buttoned his coat. Striker, leaning over in the saddle, stared at Yale's waistband where the butt of the .44 curved against his flat stomach.

"I hate to say it, Braden," Striker muttered. "But you're a plain damn fool."

"Probably."

"You done something the bunch of us should've done together. Who got shot?"

"Cliff DeLong's dead," Yale said.

"Amen," said one of the men behind him. "Maybe Larry will rest a little easier in his grave."

After they had ridden some distance, Yale turned to see dust golden against the town lights. He faced around again, the wind cool against his face. His clothing reeked of gunpowder. His nerves jumped.

"Bill, I feel like a smoke."

Slowing their horses, Striker passed over tobacco and papers. When Yale had fashioned himself a smoke and lit it with a match scraped on the horn, Striker said quietly, "So you did have a gun buried at the bottom of your trunk after all."

"I used Byerly's gun. I thought it only fitting. I should have used Larry Arthur's. But I didn't think of it in time."

CHAPTER FOURTEEN

In his own bed at Rafter A Mark Ashfork savored what he considered to be a miracle. He'd had his men bring him out here from Rincon, because he no longer wanted to stay in town, where some of the citizens were wagering as to the hour of his passing from this world. And there was always someone hammering on his hotel door, inquiring after his health. When he knew damned well they all hoped he'd die.

And he'd been there in bed when Yale Braden tried to see him. Maybe, Mark conceded on second thought, Braden didn't wish him dead. Because Braden wanted twenty thousand in gold for his 88.

His business with Braden wasn't finished yet. Maybe Braden thought so, but it was a long way from being done. Things had changed mightily in these past hours.

When he thought of the wedding ceremony at Pete Hatcher's ranch, his mouth turned bitter. It was the rankest sort of insult that Lucinda Channa had refused to put on a dress. And then she would not let him kiss her afterwards which, damn it, anybody knows is part of the ceremony. But the thing that had galled him the most was the fact that she started to pull the wedding band from her finger even before the door closed on her.

Mark Ashfork remembered how the wagon driven by Pop Grimsby had jolted him after leaving the Hatcher place. Then, as the morning light grew stronger, Mark had struggled to his elbows there on the pile of blankets in the wagon bed. Finally he got his back braced against the sideboards. It was then he had noticed on that memorable morning that the pain of his wound had eased off.

Tensely he probed his side, felt of the bandage. A sudden realization swept over him. He knew he still lived only because the horn of that steer had missed his lung after all.

He thought of the enraged beast that had charged him after goring his Apaloosa. With the horn tip crashing into his chest, Mark had somehow managed to shoot the animal dead by placing a shot in the left eye.

He knew he had not lost any of his powers. Power to

fight off adversaries. Power to love a woman. And now he felt a growing resolve when he thought of Lucinda Channa, and remembered the scorn in her eyes.

That morning Mark Ashfork said under his breath, "I've never had a son."

He thought of all his brothers. Duel the only one left. The others dead in Texas. Duel too mean to marry. It was one of the reasons they had left Texas.

The daughter of a neighbor forty miles south along the river. And the father and the brothers bringing her in a buggy. Demanding Duel take her as wife. And they had a scared preacher with them. Much as Mark himself had when he went to the Hatcher place to marry Lucinda Channa. Only there had not been the same reason for urgency as in Duel's case. Lucinda was not with child.

Back in Texas there had been harsh words and gunshots and two men lay dead. Duel had fled Texas.

Mark thought of all this in the wagon that morning he had become a bridegroom. And the urge to live took a new hold on him as he lay there listening to the creak of harness leather from the team, the sway and groan of the wagon as wheels dipped into ruts.

That morning he was reminded of his own turbulent life; perhaps because he had come so close to losing that life in these past hours.

He thought of their mother who had outlived their father by many years. A matriarch. He could still hear Stella Ashfork's dominating voice. There had been little affection between them. But then he supposed it had been an era of harsh living and the times had shaped her. The frontiers were not easy, with President Houston bellowing in one breath for annexation to the United States, then extending his hand to England in the next. Those years when Houston did not bow to political pressure and put to death the captured General Santa Anna he had so gloriously defeated at the battle of San Jacinto. He let Santa Anna live to once again set the borders aflame.

Added to this the Indian put this torch and scalp knife to bloody work. These roving bands of marauders intent on the annihilation of the white man, who honored treaties only among his own kind and even then not always fairly.

Mark supposed their mother had had no choice. She had to be strong to raise her sons. And it had been up to Mark, the eldest, to see that her wishes were carried out. Because of the business of raising cattle and trying to keep them all

76

alive on the frontier after the death of their father, Mark had had no time to give serious consideration to the taking of a wife.

That wedding morning in the wagon he had clenched his fists, broken nails digging into his palms. Now at long last he had a wife. And he hadn't meant it to be done by trickery. He had intended it as a final weapon against Duel; to leave a widow in control of the Rafter A.

Mark had been convinced, until the moment he had seen Lucinda trying to pull the ring from her finger, that he would surely die.

From that moment on he was certain, by God, that he wouldn't die. Not now when the future held such promise. She would bear him sons who would carry his name. What other purpose for man to be on earth? It was how a man remained alive, long after he was gone, by the implanting of his seed.

At last on that morning the wagon drew up in the alley behind the Gadsen House in Rincon. Grimsley tied the team, and the Reverend Burkhalter hurried away to go about his business of salvation.

When Grimsby hobbled up to help Mark Ashfork from the wagon, he was shouldered aside. Mark slid painfully to the ground, clung to the tailgate a moment on shaking legs. Then, as the deaf cook stared, Mark Ashfork managed by sheer will to make it into the hotel. Even so he had to pause for breath every few feet. The bandage under his sweated shirt itched mightily.

Reaching his room he flung himself on his bed, thankful that at this early hour no one had apparently witnessed his exhibition. He'd let them know in good time, damn their eyes.

He had gasped for breath, pain causing him to lock his teeth in a fierce grin. It had been a test to see if he could possibly negotiate the distance from the alley to his bed. And he had made it.

Yale Braden had spoken one truth: "They say that you can do anything you set your mind to."

Mark Ashfork knew it was his own indomitable will that had at least partially overcome the results of the savage thrust of the steer horn into his chest.

Of all the sons, those living, those dead, he alone had inherited the stamina, the courage of their mother.

Beckoning Grimsby over to the bed, Mark Ashfork laboriously wrote on a sheet of paper, *Go fetch my wife*.

Grimsby nodded his gray head that he understood.

When the cook had gone on his mission Duel entered

the room, the thinned yellow gaze studying the man on the bed.

"You think you can beat me, by marrying the Channa girl?" Duel smiled.

"So you know about it."

"I followed you last night. This morning I made Pete Hatcher tell me what had gone on in his house."

"You put a knife at his throat," Mark said, his eyes hard.

Duel laughed. "Not exactly."

"I'm going to disappoint you, brother. I'm not going to die."

Duel lost his smile. "You've sent for a doctor and he's told you?"

Mark Ashfork shook his head. "I just know in my own mind I won't die." He inched up on the pillows. "Now that you're here I have something to say. Keep them Mex cows off Rafter A grass."

"Maybe you never stopped to think. The crew's loyal to me, not you."

Mark Ashfork gave his younger brother a thin smile. "Something you didn't stop to think about. That crew is loyal to the man who pays 'em. That's me."

"I'll give each man a cut of the beef—"

"A man likes cows when he can't get money. I'll give 'em money. Every man, a bonus this year. I can burn money for a week in a big bonfire, Duel. And still have plenty left."

Duel's dark face was still for a moment. "Maybe we shouldn't fight each other all the time. Maybe I can forget that you didn't ransom me outa that Mex prison—"

"I don't give a damn whether you forget it or not."

Duel came to the foot of the bed. "You always held it against me because I was Momma's favorite."

Mark's eyes flew wide, then narrowed. Right where Duel stood now was where Momma had stood that night she told him to mend his ways. Sweet Jesus, was this true? Did he hate Duel because of Momma? No, that wasn't so. Duel was a snake and for years Mark had protected him. But then he had learned Duel was a thief.

However, Duel had jolted him with his reference to Momma. Of course, Mark knew Duel had always been her favorite.

"Now that you made it back from Mexico," Mark Ashfork said grudgingly, "I'll give you another chance. But you got to do things my way."

"What do you mean, your way?"

"Next time there's a man like Byerly to deal with, I'll give the orders, not you. Understand?"

Duel shrugged. "How about Yale Braden? We just let him keep that chunk of the valley all to himself?"

"I'll handle Braden when—certain things are settled."

"How about them Mex cows, Mark? They've done grazed out the land where I been holdin' 'em. And you get your mule blood up when I mention pushin' 'em onto Rafter A."

"You steal them cows?"

"Not exactly. I'm in shares with some Mexicans." Duel spread his hands. "Of course when we get things settled around here—Won't be the first Mexicans that just sort of disappeared."

"You got to mend your ways, Duel. Momma wouldn't like it none."

"No, maybe she wouldn't," Duel conceded. "But them cows'll make us an almighty big pile of money, Mark."

"I oughta be able to set a saddle in a week. Then I'll have a look at that herd." Mark was tiring, but he tried not to show it. "Keep it quiet a few days about me takin' a wife."

"If you want it that way, Mark."

"I do. And you watch the men. No cussin' where she can hear, understand."

"She goin' to live at Rafter A?"

"I sent Grimsby for her."

When Duel had gone Mark Ashfork closed his eyes. Damn it, he was tired. The jawing with his brother had taken something out of him. What he needed most was his wife.

But she didn't come, even when he had himself moved out to the ranch. He supposed she was delayed because a woman had some packing to do.

This was what he wanted to think. But deep inside he knew different. His eyes when he glared at the ceiling were laced with raw red lines.

And then the whole thing had started to come apart. The red-bearded Eddie Toll, stiffened up from a bullet slice on his right side, came into Mark's room.

"Yale Braden just killed Cliff DeLong."

"The hell you say."

"He knocked me flat with a bullet, so's I dropped my gun. And he beefed Santo with a gun barrel. Real bad."

"How many men did Braden have with him?"

Toll's mouth tightened behind its screening of red beard. "He was alone. But he jumped us when our backs was turned."

79

"I find that damn hard to believe."

When Toll had gone, Pop Grimsby entered and wrote on a piece of paper, *Your wife is at Braden's.*

* * * * *

The news of Cliff DeLong's death was a shock to Duel. But he only let it bother him for a moment. He told Charlie Santo, whose face looked as if a horse had walked on it, "We'll just keep on like we planned."

"I'll kill that goddam Braden."

"There's plenty of time, Charlie. Plenty of time. I aim to put them cows of mine on good grass. We'll start with the hill bunch. Then we'll come back and sweep up Yale Braden."

"In town there's talk that maybe that Larry Arthur business was too raw—"

"We didn't do it, Charlie. It was the Peters bunch from the hills."

Santo was feeling of his front teeth. It was a wonder he hadn't lost them all. That sneak blow by Braden had really caught him flat-footed.

Duel said, "By the way. Any bonus Mark mentions, I'll double."

"But the boys know you got no money, only cows—"

"You never know how things'll turn out, Charlie. Hell, I might even marry my brother's widow." Throwing back his head, Duel burst into laughter.

CHAPTER FIFTEEN

In the darkness at 88 they buried Larry Arthur on a green knoll. Lucy Channa had come down from the house, a shawl over her pale hair. They had no Bible, but she quoted Scripture in a strong voice. When she had finished Yale threw in the first shovelful of dirt.

Then he walked with her, away from the knoll and the grave that the others were filling in. Unconsciously he slipped an arm about her waist and she did not draw away.

When they reached the porch, she said, "I remember when Larry Arthur first came here. He had a wife and—and so many fine plans."

"His was a brutal death."

"You're a good man, and I hoped this country would not put its blood-red brand on you as it has on the rest of us."

"A man runs for so long. Then he has to make a stand. Or he is no longer a man."

"Maybe I wish I could believe that."

She opened the door, and looked around at him. "It's still an eye for an eye, isn't it, Yale?"

"I hope one day men will learn to live together. Until then there will always be the greedy ones. And I guess you can't win a battle unless you make a show of strength."

"Strength takes money. My father lost his." Her voice broke. "That's when Rafter A killed him."

She sounded so forlorn that he put out his arms and she came against him. He could feel her tremble as she wept against his chest. Then, with a small cry, she twisted away and ran into the house.

That night sleep was elusive. He heard his men talking in low tones in the dark. Striker had set out guards, and there was an air of tension in the bunkhouse.

In the morning Yale went to the south pasture to work off some of his tensions by taking the fire out of a blaze-faced roan he was trying to break to saddle. At the same time he tried to plan what to do next. The killing of DeLong would make Rafter A hard to handle.

When he had ridden the horse down he swung it toward

the gate. Striker was there, an unlighted cigarette between his lips.

"You're an almighty gutty man, Yale," Striker said. "And I'm sorry I doubted you. We heard how it happened. All of it."

Yale patted the sweated barrel of the roan. "Who told you?"

"Drifter come through. He was in town last night. You braced not only DeLong, but Santo and Toll. After this, let us side you, Yale."

Yale tried to smile. "At least one thing was accomplished. You've suddenly remembered that I have a first name."

At noon Thela arrived at 88 in a buggy driven by a hostler from the Rincon Stables. In an ice blue gown she seemed coldly angered. The wind had torn her dark hair loose from its pins.

Stepping from the buggy, she confronted him. "There is a rumor that you have Mark Ashfork's wife here!"

"She's a woman who carries the Ashfork name," Yale said quietly. "She's not his wife. She never will be."

"Why do you take it upon yourself to side her?"

"Because she has no one else to turn to."

Thela turned her head and began to weep. Yale did not beg her to stop, as was his custom. He just stared at the buggy where the hostler, smoking a cigar, was holding in the team.

Finally, when Yale did not speak, Thela said in a tremulous voice, "Are you trying to ruin everything for us?"

"Ruin everything? Just how?"

"Why did you so brazenly shoot Cliff DeLong?"

"Because he brazenly killed one of my men!"

"And who was your man? Just a cowhand. You were going to sell out. Your men would have drifted. What concern—"

"I used to think there was a world of difference between you and your father. Now I'm not so sure."

"If you're implying that my father feels the same way, you're right."

"I'm not surprised."

"He feels you should not have interfered." And when she saw the hardening of Yale's mouth, she looked a little anxious. "Don't you see, honey, it just makes his job that much harder?"

"I can imagine," Yale said dryly.

"Rafter A is going to demand that something be done—"

"Demand! Is your father Rafter A's private sheriff?"

She walked away for a few yards then turned when he caught up with her. "How could you do this to me? After we sealed our betrothal—"

"So far as I'm concerned nothing has changed. Only our plans are different. We're going to California as I originally intended."

"Well, I don't intend—" Thela broke off, her face turning crimson. Lucy Channa was hurrying down the path from the house, her sheaf of pale hair swaying across her back. Then as Thela regarded her coldly, Lucy slowed, obviously embarrassed.

"Thela, I just thought I should explain my presence here—"

Thela looked her over. "Miss Lucinda Channa, heiress from New Mexico, late of Miss Darlington's Academy, St. Louis."

"Thela, why are you so bitter?"

"I made a mistake. It's Mrs. Mark Ashfork. Why don't you go to your husband? Instead of sharing another man's house!"

Yale said, "Thela, that's quite enough."

Lucy Channa stared at Thela, biting her lip. "We were such friends when we were younger—"

"When you had everything. And I had—" Thela's mouth trembled. "Yale, are you going to order her off this ranch?"

"No. She'll leave in her own good time."

Thela gathered her skirts. "Mark will be furious when he learns you have been dallying with his wife—"

Lucy Channa flushed. "That was a vile accusation, Thela."

Thela laughed shrilly. "Yale, what will people say, when they learn you and this woman—"

"I don't give a damn what people say!"

Lucy Channa gave him a strange look. Then, although he called to her, she hurried back up the path to the house, her back stiff. The slamming of the door sounded like a gunshot.

Thela tried a new approach, as if hoping to ease the strain between them. "Darling, you risk so much by letting her stay here." And when Yale made no reply, she held out her arm. "You may escort me back to the buggy."

She seemed surprised when he followed her suggestion, instead of trying to heal the breach. And as they walked together, she looked up at him. "Yale, honey, father has talked to Duel and Mark. He's going to see they hold off until you are off this ranch and in the Gadsen House—"

He halted, feeling a raw anger. "We're going to California."

"Yale, that isn't fair—to me."

Yale walked her to the buggy. "I'll see you in town. After we've both cooled off."

When the buggy swung back along the road through the aspens, Yale saw Thela lean out and flutter a white handkerchief at him. He lifted his hand and walked down to where Bill Striker was examining some horseshoes.

Yale gestured at the low-lying hills, thick with timber; the higher peaks jutting beyond. "We wouldn't stand much chance if Rafter A bottled us up here."

Striker nodded. "Our best chance is to get some help. Larry Arthur was one of the Peters clan. So was Byerly. Maybe old man Peters will feel kindly toward you now for killin' Delong."

"I wish we could have settled this thing peacefully."

"Can't be done when you deal with somebody like Duel. He's held himself in since he come back, but—"

"You call shooting Byerly and killing Arthur holding himself in?"

Striker spat a shred of tobacco clinging to his lower lip. "Duel didn't do it himself, he had it done. When he starts doin' things himself, we'll have hell in a bright red basket."

CHAPTER SIXTEEN

Yale went to the house and tried to see Lucy Channa, but she refused to open the door. She said she was tired.

"But I want to discuss your trip to Mesilla," Yale said.

"Later, if you wish," she said stiffly through the door.

As he turned back down the path he told himself that Thela coming here had upset her. Well, he'd have a talk with her tonight. If things shaped up as he sensed they would, she needed a place of safety.

An hour later Pop Grimsby, the Rafter A cook, approached the yard, riding a mule. When the old man reined in he purposely kept his hands wide of his body, so no one could misunderstand his peaceful mission. He handed Yale a note.

> Braden: You hold property of mine.
> My wife. Grimsby will collect same
> and bring her where she belongs.
> M. Ashfork

Angrily Yale crumpled the note. "He calls a woman his property! Just who in hell does Mark think he is, God?"

Then he remembered Grimsby was deaf. He borrowed a pencil from Striker and wrote his own note to send back with Grimsby.

> Mark Ashfork: It's a woman's right to
> make her own choice.
> Yale Braden

When Grimsby had gone, Yale said, "Bill, that girl's not really Mark's wife. He should realize it."

"Be somethin' if he didn't die after all."

"If he doesn't, he'll be as great a threat to us as Duel."

"How does California look to you now, Yale?"

"It's too damn far away to even think about . . . Bill, how many able bodied men do you think Peters has?"

"A dozen, maybe."

"Doesn't cut the odds much, but it helps. We'd better go and see him and form a mutual plan for defense."

Telling the men to keep their eyes open, Yale and his foreman rode up through the archway of trees, where shadows were deep. As the trail climbed, Yale looked around. It was in such a place as this that the ambusher had tried to kill him. He wished there had been time at Madam Telfer's to have gone into the matter further with DeLong.

As was his habit whenever he thought of that narrow margin of life, Yale took a deep breath. The air tasted of life. It was good. He would have his talk with Thela and straighten things out. The fact that he had survived his wound at all was due in part to Thela's nursing him, with the help of her servant, Luz Camacho. Thela was fickle, determined, but perhaps these were traits a man should expect in a woman. At that moment Lucy Channa crossed his mind.

"I've suddenly realized I like this country, Bill. It nearly took my life. But it also—"

The sound of a distant shot rattled down through the clear air.

Striker reined in. "Might be somebody after a deer."

They listened. Two more quick shots, then a third, this a rifle of heavier caliber.

"The last one sounds like a Sharps," Striker said.

The silence clamped down. Then followed two more shots, widely spaced. The heavy rifle boomed again.

"Somebody's in trouble, that's for certain," Yale said. "If it was the war, I'd swear some of my boys had a sniper treed."

As they pushed forward, Striker cautioned, "We better go easy. No tellin' what we'll run into up there."

Shots came again as they kept their mounts at a lope. When the trail steepened they were forced to slowdown. Rifle fire crackled nearer now, but the heavier weapon no longer made its thunderous sound. A revolver began a steady fire, to be answered by the rifles.

The trail twisted, dipped and climbed again. At last they reached a ridge that overlooked a small valley. Timber grew thickly around a meadow below. In the center of the grassy sweep were two dead horses. Near one of the mounts a man lay on his face, his arms and legs twisted awkwardly. He didn't move. But the man who had taken refuge behind the other dead horse was very much alive. He looked young and rangy and was firing a revolver at men concealed in the woods directly ahead of him.

Striker was leaning over the horn. "The live one looks like Eph Peters. An' I think that's old Jer himself layin' on the ground there."

Yale caught another movement far across the meadow. Two men were sneaking in, trying to get behind Eph Peters.

That meant four against him, two in front and another pair trying to cut him down from the rear.

"It's a good guess the boys with the rifles are Rafter A," Yale said. "And if we don't help that Peters kid, he'll have that yonder pair shooting at his back in another minute."

Drawing booted rifles, they cut down through the woods, recklessly exposing themselves. When they were in range they began firing into the thicket where Eph Peters was directing his own shots. Although they could not see their target the fusillade had the desired effect. Yale saw two men in big hats break from the thicket and run toward some horses about forty feet deeper in the woods.

"It's Rafter A all right!" Striker shouted, and fired again.

One of the men stumbled, fell against a horse. The mount kicked at him. The man went down. The other one climbed into the saddle. He squeezed off a shot that went whining overhead. He shouted something to the man who was down, but the man made no response. Bent over the horn, the other one spurred for his life.

A rattle of shots from the second pair came at Eph Peters' back. But Peters, aware that help was at hand, vaulted over the dead horse and took refuge on this, the near side.

"Hang on!" Yale shouted.

Eph nodded that he understood and tried to reach the two Rafter A men with his revolver, but they were out of range.

However, Yale and Bill Striker laid down a scorching rifle fire that flushed the Rafter A men and sent them running for their horses. Yale pulled in, sighted his rifle and fired. A high-crowned hat sailed off a bald head. Now the two Rafter A men, no longer hidden by the trees, burst into sight, flogging their horses over a rise. Then they dropped from sight.

"Must have thought we were a small army," Yale observed, reloading.

When they swung across the meadow Eph was turning over the body of Jeremiah Peters. Yale's mouth hardened as he saw the gray beard spotted with blood.

"They killed Uncle Jer," Eph said disconsolately. He picked up a Sharps rifle that had fallen beside the leader of the hill clan. "Uncle Jer was doin' right well with this afore he run outa shells. I busted my own rifle when my hoss piled up."

"If we only had a decent sheriff—" Striker broke off, then glanced at Yale.

"Bill, I agree," Yale thinly. "Josh Wheatley is a sorry sheriff. Damn sorry."

Eph Peters was staring at the body of his uncle. "I feel bad about Uncle Jer, but he always said when it come his time to go, he wanted it to be a shootin' kind of goin'."

Yale bit back an oath at the senseless killing of this old man. "We were on our way to see your uncle," Yale told Eph. "To discuss defending ourselves against Rafter A. A little late, I guess."

Yale rode over to where the Rafter A man Striker had shot had been thrashing around in the brush. The man was dead. Yale led the Rafter A horse to the meadow where they tied on the old man's body. Eph Peters swung up behind Striker and they pushed deeper into the mountains.

"How'd they jump you, anyway?" Striker asked.

"Me an' Uncle Jer was just ridin' home an' there they was. Shootin'. The hosses got it right then. One of them fellas shouted they aimed to hang us. Said we was rustlers. But we fought back an' reckon they figured it was best to take no chances an' shoot us to pieces."

They climbed a ridge and at last came to a plateau. Ahead, woodsmoke stained the sky through the trees. And finally they heard the neigh of horses above the wind. Something about the solemn way they approached alerted the occupants of the stone and log huts Yale could see strung out across the clearing. A cluster of men came from the corrals and barns, most of them bearded. All armed. Already some of the women started to wail, for they could see the bearded body on the led horse.

Eph used his own knife to cut the body from the Rafter A horse. He carried his uncle into the largest of the log houses and placed the body on a long plank table. The hill people drifted in to stare.

A stony-eyed old woman came from a back room. As she approached the body there was a noticeable trembling of her lips. But by some summoning of will she seemed to regain control.

"Jer, the blue-belly Yanks couldn't kill you. You had to come all the way to New Mexico to get your coffin."

Yale had seen the woman once in town, the widow of Jeremiah Peters. Yale said, "I'm sorry your husband had to die."

The old woman drew tighter a ragged gray shawl across her shoulders. She lifted bitter eyes to Yale. "It's because of you that Jer's dead."

"Wait, Aunt Tillie," Eph protested. "You don't understand."
But the old woman silenced him with a lift of her bony hand.

"Maybe Rafter A would've kept away from us, Braden,"
she said harshly, "if you hadn't come here. Jer said we was
to leave you alone. You was from Missouri, Jer said, and
some good boys come from there. Even if you did fight for
the Nawth."

"I appreciate his feelings—"

She took a step toward Yale, away from the dead man on
the table. "You damn blue-belly, I could kill you myself."

Her voice ended in a shriek. Turning, she snatched a
pistol from the belt of one of the men. But before she could
fire it, Eph tore the weapon from her fingers. The others
made no move to interfere. They stood, watching, hands
clamped to their weapons. In the yard a dog howled.

"You got to listen, Aunt Tillie!" Eph cried. "It ain't Braden's fault Uncle Jer's dead. If him and Striker hadn't come
along them Rafter A killer would've done me in too."

But the nephew's words did not lessen the anger in the
old woman's eyes. "Blue-belly, you git," she said fiercely.
"Don't come back here. Never."

"I hoped we could stand together." Yale looked around at
the tight faces of the armed men. They just stared, and
finally Yale said, "Bill, we'd best get out of here."

Eph followed Yale and Striker outside, holding the revolver
he had taken from the old woman. "Now that Uncle Jer's
gone, the rest will likely listen to what she says. But I'll talk
to her. I'll do my best."

Striker swung into the saddle. "Reckon the old lady will be
running things. At least for awhile. Until Jeremiah's death
sort of wears off on 'em."

Two men had come out of the house to stare. "If we
don't all stand together in this," Yale told them darkly, "maybe there won't be any left who care whether it wears off or
not."

By the time they reached home it was nearly dark.

Alex Beacham, in the cookshack, took a quick drink from
a bottle then hid it behind a sack of flour. He hurried to the
yard where Yale Braden and Striker were dismounting.

"Didn't figure to let her go," the cook panted, his eyes
apologetic. "But she said it was her business and we
wasn't to stop her."

Yale, tired from the long ride, depressed over Jeremiah
Peters' death, which seemed to eliminate any alliance with
the hill crowd, did not comprehend immediately. Then his

89

face tightened. "Her? What in hell are you talking about?"

"Miss Channa or Mrs. Ashfork, however you like. Said she left you a note at the house."

Back in the saddle, Yale jammed in the spurs so hard the tired horse squealed. In front of the house he reined in sharply, scattering pebbles against the steps. When he flung himself inside, he was aware instantly of the empty house. Numbly he crossed over to peer at the square of white paper anchored to the tabletop with a cartridge.

> Mr. Braden: I am going to Mesilla.
> When I am settled I will ask you to
> send my portmanteau. I will see that
> your horse is returned.
>
> > Lucinda Channa.

Crumpling the note he flung himself outside. Striker was coming up the path. "The little fool," Yale cried. "She shouldn't be out alone in country like this."

"Mebbe not," Striker put in when Yale explained. "But the Channas always did have a mule head when they made up their minds. You aim to go after her?"

"I aim," Yale said through his teeth. Turning to the nearest man he yelled, "Saddle me a fresh horse!"

After filling his pockets with rifle shells, wolfing slices of cold meat, he got further details from Beacham.

"She said somethin' about the way station at Half Pine," the cook volunteered.

Yale struck out alone through the pass. Within a mile twilight thickened into night. Stars were dull in a gunmetal sky. The moon rode the early night on the other side of the world; here there would be no light for hours. He lost all sense of time in his urgency to reach the girl before she might run into trouble. Finally he saw a dot of light and knew what it was. For miles Yale watched the single yellow eye of the window at the way station hang like a flaring match head on the horizon.

Much later he came down a canyon and there was the sod-roofed station with its corrals for stage stock, used when fresh teams were needed to make the grade into Rincon. On the southbound Mesilla run the station was bypassed unless there were passengers to take on. As he approached he saw that the place was dark. Either his eyes had played tricks and he imagined he saw a lighted window, or someone had blown out a lamp. Loosening his gun, he rode down.

He swung wearily out of the saddle and pounded on

the heavy door. At last he saw a shard of yellow as a lamp was lighted.

A sleepy voice said, "No vittles or drinks this time of night. And the Mesilla stage has already gone. Be on your way—"

"I'm Yale Braden of Eighty-Eight. Was the Channa girl here?"

"Yep. Took the Mesilla stage. She left a hoss for you."

"Open up."

"Now listen, Braden—" But Yale hammered so loudly on the thick panel, the voice said, "All right—wait." A bolt slid out of its socket and the door swung open.

Yale stared at Si Olcutt, operator of the station. The fat face, ringed by a fringe of gray hair, was worried. Olcutt wore pants and underwear with galluses hanging.

Something in Yale's eye, catching light from a lamp on a shelf, made Olcutt say, "God's truth. I ain't lyin' about the girl."

"She took the Mesilla stage?"

"The very one."

Turning, Yale stared out the doorway at the darkened road that twisted off into the night. A faint odor of dust still hung in the air.

"How many passengers?" Yale demanded suddenly, facing around.

"Three. Two men and a woman. She'll be safe enough, Braden. I hear you're goin' to buy the Gadsen House."

"You heard wrong."

"How about that hoss she left?"

"I don't feel like leading it all the way home tonight. I'll send a man for it."

Even though Lucy Channa seemed safe enough, Yale felt a nagging apprehension. As he started back for 88 he looked around. The door to the way station was closed, the window dark. Well, it was Lucy's decision to go to Mesilla. And there was no doubt that she would be safer there than at 88. The crisis had deepened with the death of Jeremiah Peters.

Now that he had declared himself in the fight, he felt a quickening of his pulse. Even though he still deplored killings he found that since making up his mind to stand up for his rights, he found a new zest for life.

As he rode into the darkness he wondered if some of this new awareness was not due to meeting Lucy Channa. And he found himself anticipating the day he would personally deliver her portmanteau to Mesilla. But then a shard of guilt touched his mind. He was being unfair to Thela.

CHAPTER SEVENTEEN

Only when Yale Braden's horse could no longer be heard did the hand come free of Lucy Channa's mouth. The hand was large and tasted of leather reins and gun oil and sweat. Now that he had released her she drew away from Charlie Santo in the darkened room. She sensed rather than heard him ease down the hammer of his rifle.

"I should've killed him anyhow," Santo grunted. "For what he done to my face."

Pete Hatcher's voice sounded reedy in the darkness. "That wouldn't have been right. I promised Lucy there'd be no shooting."

"Just the same I kept my hand on her mouth," Santo said. "If she'd let out a squeak— That goddam Braden. He's got luck. Too much of it. The way he handled DeLong. Kee-rist, that blue-belly—"

Lucy Channa rubbed at her lips where Santo had held his hand. "Uncle Pete, I'll never forgive you for this."

Pete Hatcher said, "You're Mark's wife. You got a duty—"

Olcutt, holding a lamp, put his head in the door. "Never figured Braden would get here this soon. Scared me. That was close."

"Close for Braden," Santo muttered, his big body stiff with anger. Lamplight touched the wound that slanted across his face. "You better ride with us peaceful, Mrs. Ashfork."

Lucy said nothing. She was afraid if she put up a fight now, Santo would go after Braden and kill him. Just to get even with her. No, she couldn't risk it.

Everything had gone so wrong tonight. She had arrived here hours ago, hardly dressed for passage on a stage. But that couldn't be helped. The moment she had appeared Olcutt seemed surprised to see her. When she told him about wanting to catch the Mesilla stage, he said she should rest, because it wouldn't arrive till midnight. As long as the weather was good the stage wouldn't lay over for the night. Olcutt let her have a small room furnished with a cot and chair. Then he locked her in. The window was too small for escape. She heard Olcutt talking to his hostler. Rafter A was mentioned.

She knew now the hostler had ridden to Rincon. Charlie Santo was the only Rafter A man in town. But her uncle happened to be in Quincy's Saloon. He and Santo came for her, arriving not five minutes before Yale Braden.

Then they had heard the sound of an approaching rider and Santo had blown out the lamp.

Olcott whispered from the front window, "By God, it's Braden."

And Uncle Pete said nervously, "Lucy, you keep your mouth shut or Braden will get hurt."

"Hurt bad," Santo grunted. In one hand he held a cocked rifle. The other hand he clapped over her mouth.

But now Braden had left, thinking she was on the stage.

Olcutt loaned one of his saddlers. Her uncle forced her into the saddle. For a moment she considered some desperate move. But this was not the time to make a break, she told herself. An outcry, a gunshot might bring Braden. He had treated her decently. She didn't want anything to happen to him. They rode out into the night.

Uncle Pete said, "You should've knowed you couldn't take a stage without word gettin' to Rafter A."

Lucy gave a shaky laugh. "How much reward did Olcutt earn for my hide?"

"A hundred dollars out of my own pocket," Pete Hatcher said. "Money I can't afford."

"Undoubtedly," she said coldly, "you will be reimbursed by Rafter A."

Santo said, "Less talk and more ride. We got a long way to go."

The moon slid over the Mogollons, and brightened the velvet sky. The trail climbed, dipped, climbed.

And when they paused to let the horses blow, Lucy said, "I feel faint." She swayed in the saddle.

When Santo reined close to see what was the matter, she made a desperate try for his holstered revolver. But he was too quick. With an oath he slapped her hand away. Her other hand shot up, nails raking into the fresh scars that Yale Braden's revolver had put on his face. Santo roared with pain and rage. The horse reared.

Hatcher cried, "Don't let her get away."

As Lucy rammed in the spurs a heavy arm swept around her waist with such pressure the wind was knocked out of her. For an instant she hung limp against the flank of Santo's

93

horse while her own mount went pounding off into the darkness. She felt herself drawn across a saddle. Forcing her eyes open she peered up. Through a tangle of her hair that had come free, she saw the face of Santo above her. The light was so strong here in the open she could see the ugly marks left on his face by her nails.

Leaning down he whispered, "You bitch. If you wasn't married to Mark Ashfork. If I didn't have five hundred iron dollars waiting for me when I deliver you—"

"Turn me loose!" When she tried to claw his face, the voice of Charlie Santo froze her.

"Try that again and I'll kick your uncle in the head. And to hell with Mark Ashfork. To hell with five hundred dollars."

She ceased struggling. She knew he meant what he said.

It took some minutes for her uncle to run down the spooked horse she had been riding.

At last he rode up, leading the animal. "Save your wildcat temper for Mark," her uncle said. "Looks like she clawed you, Santo."

Santo was dabbing at his face with a bandanna. He stowed the bandanna and swung her to the ground. They started riding again.

For the first time in her life she felt a real, shaking fear. Each time she saw Santo turn in the saddle to stare at her, she went cold. She wondered bitterly if Santo decided to do as he threatened, how much of a defender her uncle would be. Not much, she decided.

This Pete Hatcher who had made her feel obligated to her relatives, so she would marry a dying man.

But the man had not died.

Closing her eyes she felt tears whipped dry against her cheeks by the night wind. Why had she left 88 and tried to go it alone? Why hadn't she admitted to Braden her true feelings? Why hadn't she spoken her mind, told him what a terrible wife Thela would make any man. She thought of how Braden had slipped his arm about her waist as they walked to the house after the burial of Larry Arthur. A strong man, Braden, who did not like violence. But who had been forced into it.

Why did she not have such a man for herself?

Later her uncle pointed to distant lights. "Rafter A."

Nearness of the ranch frightened her. Once at Rafter A she knew what would be expected of her. Panic shook her. But she forced herself to speak with resignation.

"Uncle Pete, it will almost be a relief to get it over with."

Santo, riding ahead, looked around and laughed. Her uncle's lank figure stiffened as he swung close to peer at her in the darkness. As if wary of her apparent change in attitude.

Then, as if assured of her mood, he slapped her affectionately on the arm. "I knew you'd see your duty." His voice grew tense with bright promise. "Why, just think what it'll mean to us all. You bein' Mark's wife—"

This time she did not attempt to snatch a revolver. This time she reined suddenly away, driving in the spurs so that her pony squealed. Santo, in trying to swing quickly and intercept her, slammed into her uncle's mount. Both horses nearly lost footing. There were shrill cries of rage from Hatcher, cursing from Santo.

As she swept deeper into the dark hills she could hear them pounding after her. But at a fork in the trail, she drove her tired horse into a thicket. Santo and her uncle swept on past her hiding place. It was much later that she started to make her way through the hills; country she had known all her life. She did not allow herself to think what might happen if Santo caught her out alone. Was there much choice, after all, between Santo or the bull-necked rancher who had ordered her father hanged to a tree?

CHAPTER EIGHTEEN

As Yale neared headquarters he was challenged. It pleased him that Striker was keeping the place well guarded.

Striker came down from the bunkhouse and they talked quietly for a few moments, Yale telling how Lucy Channa had made it to the Half Pine way station and taken the stage to Mesilla. And when he finished he stared at the darkened windows of the house. Feeling empty as if a part of his life had left with the girl.

Striker said, "One of the boys seen somebody spyin' on the place just after dark. We tried to ride him down, but he got away."

Yale gave a rueful smile. "And I planned to go someplace where it was safe. I suspect that sort of place doesn't exist. At least not on this earth."

"Amen," Striker agreed.

"Rafter A is liable to hit at any time." Yale studied the towering Mogollons, jutting against the moon-swept sky. "I've got a hunch we'd better be ready."

"Know what you mean, Yale." Striker swore under his breath. "They killed Larry Arthur and old man Peters. Next they'll try to tromp the lot of us into the ground."

Many times in the war Yale had experienced an acute awareness of possible disaster. And suddenly he made up his mind. "Bill, let's clear out of here. Bring every gun and all the shells you can find. We'll pack enough provisions for four days. Have one of the men give Beacham a hand."

Within the hour they were ready to go. Upslope, but still in sight of the headquarters buildings, Yale called a halt. Yale explained the position each man was to take if trouble developed. Yale, Striker, Beacham and another rider would be posted on either side of the narrow track that angled through the aspens toward Rincon. The other four men would be stationed farther up the road.

As the hours passed Striker gave Yale a curious glance. "You just figure to let Rafter A ride in and do what they want?"

"We'll have to fight the war my way. Bill, you were on

96

the short side in the war. You had to use more strategy sometimes than we did."

"I got a hunch you don't mean to hit Rafter A on the
way in."

"I plan to hit them when they leave. They'll be expecting
us on the way in."

Yale took a turn at guard duty along with Striker The
rest of the men rolled up in their blankets.

Daylight came and still they waited. They ate cold bacon
and biscuits. Alex Beacham grumbled that at least he should
be allowed to build a small fire so he could give them hot
food. But Yale shook his head. As he chewed a biscuit he
kept watching his buildings in the clearing below. The windows were wide open, the doors ajar. No sign of activity at
all. The day wore on.

Finally, in the last flush of daylight, they heard a distant
stirring against the mountain stillness. Then Yale saw them.
Some twenty men, so confident of success they hadn't even
brought the full crew. Sight of four draft horses being herd-
ed along the road caused Striker's brows to shoot up.

"What in hell do they figure to do with them?" the foreman whispered.

"It seems," Yale answered grimly, "that they intend to do
a thorough job."

"I don't understand."

"More of an insult than burning a man out. It was done
in the war."

The Rafter A men passed, not a dozen yards away. They
went on down into the hollow. Yale had guessed right. From
the promontory they could see Duel Ashfork giving the men
their orders. Duel was tramping through the empty buildings.
Satisfied no one was around, Duel, darkly handsome, returned to the yard with an armload of Yale's books.

Yale crouched with teeth clenched as he saw other men
carrying out his books to dump them in a pile in the yard.
Then, methodically, the men tore off the covers and ripped
out pages until there was nothing left but scattered bits of
paper.

Striker whispered tensely, "How can you set there and
let 'em do that?"

"One thing I learned in the war. Patience. Sometimes
you have to take a lot in order to get in your licks."

When the books were completely destroyed Duel's voice
exploded up to them: "Get a hitch on that goddam post!"
he ordered.

One of the Rafter A men rode close, looped a chain around one of the supports of the veranda overhang. On the other end of the chain the work team strained. The post was jerked loose. Down came the overhang with a crash. Then the four horses were backed to the south wall. Chains were strung through open windows and through the doorway. This time when the team moved the wall swayed. With a screeching of nails pulled free, it collapsed. The roof was next and it teetered precariously then plunged down. This went on, with the bunkhouse, the barn. All that remained were piles of wreckage.

Alex Beacham, smelling of whisky, crept to Yale's side. The fat cook stared down incredulously at the carnage. "Why didn't they just pour on a little coal-oil and throw a torch?"

"That's too easy," Yale explained grimly. "This way hits a man in the gut. It will prove to the whole country that Rafter A could take their time to pull down my buildings and rip my books. And we couldn't do a damn thing to stop them."

Because the destruction below now seemed complete, Yale reminded his men of their orders. They stood in a circle, moonlight touching grim faces.

"Hit them hard where it counts," he reminded. "Then get the hell out. If we get separated we meet a mile this side of the Half Pine way station. Agreed?"

One of the men pointed down the road. "Here they come. Fat and lazy like they just had a summer picnic."

Yale could see the mass of riders in the moonlight. "All right, take your positions."

As four of the men scrambled up the road, Striker shook his head. "Seems we should at least stay together."

"No."

"We're makin' our ranks almighty thin, Yale."

"That's why we'll hit them and ride for it."

Striker scowled. "I hope you're right."

"We only have one alternative. To do it this way, or let them obliterate us. As they did my buildings—" Yale's voice hardened "—and my books."

Yale watched the knot of riders coming up the road. Moving leisurely with the work horses that had done the job of dismantling the house where he had lived for so many months. He felt a stab of anger that he had been forced to stand by and witness the destruction. He knew how easy it would have been to let emotions spur him into a foolish act, to have ridden down and challenged them.

Now as the Rafter A men drew closer he could see Duel Ashfork in the lead. At Duel's side rode Charlie Santo, and a little behind was a smaller man. He thought it was Eddie Toll, the man he had shot at the Telfer woman's place. It must have been only a surface wound or Toll wouldn't be in the saddle.

Yale pushed his rifle through a screening of shin oak. He could hear the stirring of the 88 horses in the woods behind them. It was Beacham's assignment to keep the mounts quiet.

As Yale felt his finger curl on the cold trigger he wondered why these things always had to end with men bleeding upon the ground. Why couldn't reason prevail? There were always people like Duel to push and badger until finally it was their life or yours.

He could hear the jingle of bit chains from the approaching horses mingled with the muted voices of the riders. Some of the men were taking their last breath. And this he regretted, no matter who it might be, because it seemed such a waste. And yet, what choice was there? It was the red clay of Virginia all over again, with men dying.

In the darkness he could not see his men, but he could hear them easing their cramped bodies. Cursing softly, some of them, as men do before battle.

Striker grunted, "I hope to kee-rist I kill Duel. It would end this thing."

"Maybe. But there's still Mark."

There was faint laughter from the group of Rafter A riders as one of them loudly commented on the wreckage below.

Another said, "I told you, Duel. That blue-belly Braden is yellow clear to his heels."

For a moment the horsemen were lost to sight where the road dipped. But now the leaders were climbing, as if from a great depression in the earth.

"Wonder where Braden went?" a rider speculated.

"Californy, so I hear."

"Well, one thing, he never married Thela Wheatley."

Yale fingered his rifle, wondering how these Rafter A men could be so careless. He knew that he had planned it right. Duel and his crew had been primed for trouble when they approached the ranch. Finding it deserted they had relaxed and gone about their business of destruction.

Yale started to straighten up. Behind him there was a sudden crash of glass deep in the brush. This followed by Beacham's involuntary cry of disgust: "Goddam, I dropped the bottle—"

The sound of the smashed bottle was more startling than a gunshot. The Rafter A riders milled, shouting.

Duel cried, "Watch it!" and fired toward the sound of Beacham's voice.

Rifle fire erupted from the brush.

Yale got off a shot at the tall shadow that was Duel Ashfork. But horses were rearing, spooked by the sudden yells, the screaming shots. A horse went down, throwing its rider. The man tried to rise but those in back rode right over him.

They came charging up the road like cavalry.

Yale's mouth was dust-dry as he squeezed off a shot. He saw another dark shape fall beneath the running horses. To his right Striker's rifle spat an orange-red finger at the riders. A man yelled in pain. And then as the Rafter A men pounded past, firing into the brush, there were more gunshots up ahead. Yale's four-men stationed there were cutting into the leaders. The screams of horses hit chilled the blood.

Yale cocked his rifle and fired again. He shouted at the mass of riders. "You didn't have to come! If you'd stayed on your own side of the fence!"

But his voice was lost in the crash of gunfire. Off in the brush a man suddenly groaned and said, "Mother of God—"

To Yale the voice sounded like Beacham's, but he couldn't be sure in the darkness and confusion. Yale's shoulder was taking the full slam of the rifle's recall. Reloading swiftly, he hissed at Striker, "Come on, let's move. Get the rest of the boys."

They ran down through the trees, away from the tangle of horses and groaning men. Those Rafter A riders still in the saddle were far up the road now. The road was littered with the dark shapes of downed horses and men.

But the Rafter A survivors had recovered from their initial surprise and were firing back down the road. A bullet smashed against an aspen trunk. Another ricocheted off a rock, making a sound that jarred the nerves. Yale could see that the bunched 88 horses were milling. His men who had been stationed up the road were plunging down, drawn by Striker's signal.

Yale jerked his reins away from a stump. Then they were riding hard for the Mogollons. Some of the Rafter A bunch came after them, but soon lost heart. They'd been hit hard and had no stomach for a further encounter with the 88 crew this night.

Later, Yale's men halted to let their horses blow. In the sudden quiet Yale looked around. There were no sounds of pursuit. "How'd we fare?" he asked.

Striker said, "Ralph here has got a cut on his arm."

"Ain't much," Ralph Jordan grunted.

Striker gave a tight laugh. "We sure hit 'em good. Even if Beacham did drop that bottle. Reckon his hands were shaking so—"

Yale was staring at the shadowed faces. "Where is Beacham?"

"By gawd, I remember hearin' a man sound like he was hit," Striker admitted.

They circled back toward the ruined 88 headquarters. By the time they reached the road they could see that the wounded had been removed. But Rafter A had not waited to bury their dead. Yale and Striker, probing the brush, finally came upon the body of the cook. Beacham had been hit twice. The second shot had finished him. Lashing the body on a horse they hit for the mountains again, in case Rafter A was coming back with reinforcements. Finally in sandy ground they scratched out a grave of sorts, buried Beacham, and covered it with rocks to keep off predators.

Yale was suddenly depressed. They had won this battle, but what would the next one bring?

They began riding silently southward in the direction of the Half Pine way station. There they could pick up news from town, and plan their next move.

All during the ride Yale's mood darkened. Whenever he thought of Lucinda Channa he felt a growing unease.

CHAPTER NINETEEN

The news that a two-bit ranch the size of 88 had literally spit in the eye of the giant Rafter A, swept the whole range. Casualties were seven Rafter A dead, four wounded. That wasn't counting the horses caught in the deadly fire. The big outfits south of Rafter A gave orders that no man was to ride alone; each man was to be fully armed at all times. The next morning Southworth of Rincon Hardware did a big business in rifles and shells. Even though some of the hill crowd tried to patronize him, he refused. He wasn't forgetting what had happened to Byerly.

Southworth, sweating behind his counter, told Josh Wheatley just how he felt about it. "Braden could have had a fine future here. Respected businessman, owner of the Gadsen House. Now he's thrown it all away. How does Thela feel about it?"

"She's some put out with him." Wheatley fingered his bristly mustache. "Funny thing, I always figured no man could build a big enough fire under Yale Braden to make him fight back."

Southworth, concluding a sale of cartridges to the segundo at the vast Running J ranch, said, "I understand Duel was on a peaceful mission. Trying to buy Braden out. And Braden ambushed him."

Wheatley took a moment to weigh his answer. "Between you and me, Ardin," the sheriff said in a low voice, "it don't sound reasonable that Duel would take twenty men—"

"Josh, I'm a little surprised at you. Defending an outlaw like Braden."

"Well, I don't want to step too high till I figure how Thela really feels. That girl is my life, Ardin—"

Southworth looked annoyed. He leaned over the counter. "Forget Thela. Look at it this way. How much business does this town get from the small outfits like Braden's? Damn little. The big outfits support Rincon. Let's not forget that, Josh."

Wheatley grunted something under his breath and tramped on down to Quincy's. A crowd of noisy drinkers ringed Duel at the bar. Duel was telling his story for the tenth time or more to newscomers. Halting by a faro layout, Wheatley listened to him.

... "Sure I was mad. How would you feel? You're ridin' along and all of a sudden them hellions cutting loose."

"How many you reckon there was, Duel?" asked one of the listeners.

Duel Ashfork, handsome, yellow-eyed, his face still streaked from sweat and powder, looked hard. "We figure they had around forty men."

"Where in hell did Braden round up a crew that size?"

Duel looked around at the crowd. "Can't you boys figure it out? The hill bunch was in with them."

"I'll be damned."

Another asked, "What happened after they 'bushed you, Duel?"

"They run for the mountains. Then me an' the boys went down and pulled Eighty-eight apart. You blame us?"

"Hell no!"

Duel said, "If you ask me, we oughta get a posse and go after 'em." Duel's gaze settled on Josh Wheatley. "How many prisoners you figure we oughta bring back, Josh?"

The sheriff gave a weak smile. "We don't want to let this thing get out of hand."

One man, brandishing a bottle, cried, "I say we oughta fix 'em like we done them two Mex hoss thieves that time. Shot one and hung the other. Remember?"

A yell went up from the crowd.

Duel grabbed a bottle, took a long drink. Then his yellow eyes sought Wheatley in the crowd. "How about it, Josh?" The saloon grew silent. "You too weak in the gut to hang Thela's bethrothed?"

All eyes were on the sheriff, waiting for him to declare himself. He clenched, unclenched his hands and the silence grew. And on Wheatley's face was the look of a man who is walking the iced edge of a precipice. He's sure to fall, one way or the other. And he damn well better pick the shortest fall.

Tension seemed to go out of Wheatley as he made up his mind. Hooking thumbs in his belt he walked up to face Duel, a spare smile working its way under the mustache.

"We'll go after Braden and the rest of them," he said.

Another shout burst from the crowd and perspiring bartenders set out more bottles.

And through Josh Wheatley's mind ran the decision he had made. He would make Thela see the light. She would have to understand. And he was sure she would, once the facts were presented. Thela was a practical girl.

Wheatley went on, "If Yale Braden doesn't happen to make it back to the jail here—well, that's his hard luck. And so far as him being Thela's bethrothed, you can forget that, Duel. Braden's gone a long step toward ruining her life." He looked right into Duel's eyes. "Its' a time for old friends to console her."

CHAPTER TWENTY

That morning Yale knew they would be after them. With or without the law. Which meant Josh Wheatley. And with Wheatley or without him, Yale guessed, would matter little in the conduct of the man-hunters. From a rise of wooded ground he studied the Half Pine way station below. He could see Olcutt feeding the stock in the corral. There seemed to be no one else around.

"We'll ride down and get that saddler Lucy Channa rode," Yale told his men. "We may need an extra horse."

Olcutt heard them coming and leaned on the fork with which he had been pitching hay. Seven men on tired horses.

Then, as they drew nearer, Olcutt stiffened. "Braden!" he cried, and hustled his fat body into the station. The front door slammed shut. Yale heard a bolt slide home.

Surprised at Olcutt's actions Yale spurred ahead. He swung down and hammered on the door. Olcutt shouted for him to go away.

"Open up!" Yale ordered.

"Go away, Braden! You ain't welcome here."

Yale frowned. He could hear Olcutt bustling around inside. Then the unmistakable thunk of a rifle being cocked. Probably Olcutt had heard about the fight at 88. The news could have come through on an early stage.

"Olcutt, I came for the horse left by the Channa girl. The fight is over and done and—"

"What fight?" came Olcutt's cautious voice through the door.

"At my place last night. We shot it out with Rafter A."

"Oh." Olcutt sounded relieved. "I thought it was on account of—" He broke off as if realizing he'd said too much. "Help yourself to the hoss, Braden."

But Yale sensed that Olcutt fearing him somehow concerned Lucy Channa's visit here. What else?

Yale's mouth tightened. Drawing back, he signaled to Striker, who had ridden up with the others. He and Striker hit the door together. It burst inward. Olcutt, standing directly behind the portal, was bowled over. As Olcutt rolled, coming to his knees, Yale snatched the rifle from his grasp. He hauled Olcutt to his feet.

"Talk," Yale said thinly. "I've got a feeling Lucy Channa didn't take the Mesilla stage after all."

Olcutt's plump face was sweating. "Braden, I—" Then, ringed by Yale's grim, heavily-armed crew, Olcutt lost his nerve. He told how word had come from Pete Hatcher that his niece wasn't to be allowed to take any stage, should she get the notion. Because she was Mark Ashfork's wife. There was a hundred dollars in it if Lucy Channa could be prevented from taking a stage and word gotten either to her Uncle Pete Hatcher or Rafter A. There were usually some Rafter A men in Rincon.

"Santo and Hatcher took the girl with them," Olcutt finished. "I was scared not to play their game. It wasn't only the money, Braden—"

"Pete Hatcher should be strung up over a hot fire for this," Yale muttered, his face white. "His own niece."

"The gal ain't blood kin to him," Striker reminded. "It's Martha Hatcher who is her real aunt. And that woman is so scairt of Pete it's a shame."

Yale took his men outside. "Bill, I'm going after the girl. Alone."

"Now that's fool talk, Yale. You was lucky when you tried it alone against DeLong—"

"I mean it," Yale declared. "One man might get to her. Anyway, I'm going to try."

Yale switched his saddle to the mount Lucy Channa had ridden to the way station. It was fresher than the bay he had pushed through the mountains, following the attack on the Rafter A riders. Although Striker again voiced his protest at the idea of Yale going alone to brace Mark Ashfork at Rafter A, Yale would not change his plans. Making sure he had extra shells for his rifle and the revolver belonging to the late gunsmith, Yale set out.

Clouds began to drift in before he had gone three miles. It turned cold and he felt a splash of moisture against his face. Keeping to the trail just below the ridge, he pushed west, keeping his eyes open for possible pursuit.

Although he had once studied the sprawling Rafter A headquarters through field glasses, he had never been invited to the place. Nor had he had any reason to see Mark Ashfork there. Mark Ashfork had let it be known that any business transacted was to be done on the few days of each month when he occupied his room at the Gadsen House in Rincon.

As Yale approached he saw many cows with the Ashfork brand. He passed heaps of ash and mounds of dirt, the site of cookfires and garbage pits of the roundup camps.

He knew full well what would happen to him if he should be trapped by any Rafter A men.

A black cloud hovered directly overhead. Suddenly it was ripped by lightning and became a bucket halved. A torrent of rain spilled down. Pulling his hatbrim low, Yale managed to keep some of the rain out of his eyes. But it soaked into his coat, and he swore at himself for not bringing a slicker. The roan shied at wind-whipped brush and rolled its eyes when thunder crashed. And Yale was forced to use more bit on the animal than he liked, in order to hold it in.

As quickly as it had come the rain stopped. When he topped a rise he saw a shaft of sunlight spilling through the clouds, to touch a collection of dwellings and barns on a plateau not a mile ahead. He was closer to Rafter A than he had ever been before.

Slowly he approached, his nerves tight. He kept to draws so as not to be skylighted. Finally he rode as close as he dared. So close he could hear the snorting of horses in one of the three corrals.

Leaving his mount back in the brush, Yale crept forward. From a vantage point he watched the yard. There seemed to be an unusual lack of activity for so large a spread. He wondered how many Rafter A men had died last night, how many wounded.

With the wind cutting his face he saw a man stroll from the bunkhouse, a pair of chaps slung over his arm. Another one, stringy, hairless, was smoking a pipe while he emptied a pan of dishwater out the door of the cookhouse.

But there was no sign of Mark or Duel. Or Lucy Channa. His worry deepened. Perhaps Mark had taken her away, temporarily. Somewhere out of reach. When he thought of the girl, trapped by the greed of the Hatchers, in Mark's hands, he felt a burgeoning rage. For so long he had suppressed the violent side of his nature, that now it came springing easily out of long-unused corners of his consciousness. When the time came he would kill Mark Ashfork for what he had done to the girl. It had been treachery from the first, no doubt about it. Mark had pretended to be badly hurt. And Mark had known all the time that his wound would never be fatal.

107

As Yale studied the layout ahead he made up his mind to ride openly into Rafter A. There seemed to be no alternative. So far as he could tell there were only two or three men about the place. Well, he'd handled bigger odds than that last night, he tried to tell himself.

Turning back toward his roan he heard the nicker of another horse straight ahead, some distance away. He shot a hand to his waistband, drawing Byerly's revolver. As he swung around a shoulder of rock he could see the horse, a pinto. And then he glimpsed a ragged, rain-soaked figure sprinting toward him out of the brush.

Instinctively he drew back the hammer of the .44, then he lowered it. This was no Rafter A man trying to take him by surprise. A boy's shirt wetly curving at a bosom, a narrow waist, and tight, storm-dampened jeans.

Lucy Channa, her long hair plastered to her skull, the ends tangled about her shoulders, rushed toward him. Before he could return the gun to his belt, she crashed into his arm, hugging it.

"I've followed you for an hour," she whispered breathlessly, wet hair tight against his face. "I was afraid to cry out. They've been hunting me—"

He could feel her shiver against him. The shirt clinging like a second skin. The jeans torn and muddied. There was a scratch on one cheek.

His smile was fierce, and he wanted to shout as he held her. "You got away from them!"

Her teeth chattering from the cold, she recounted how, night before last, she had broken away from Charlie Santo and her uncle. They had spent most of the night searching for her, then had given up.

"I was close enough to them once to hear Uncle Pete tell Santo he was going home. That I would turn up there when I got tired and hungry."

"He doesn't know you very well. What happened to Santo?"

"I was a few miles from here yesterday afternoon when I saw him ride out with Duel and some men. They had work horses with them."

"How well I know," Yale said grimly.

"I was worried sick that something had happened to you, Yale." Her nails dug into his shoulders.

He slipped his gun under his wet coat. Tilting back her head he said, "We're going to get you dry. You need a change of clothes." Just how he was going to accomplish this he didn't know at the moment.

Although his coat had taken the full onslaught of the storm, it was reasonably warm from his body. He insisted that she slip it on. It fit her like a greatcoat and they both laughed. But because of the danger that faced them both, the humor endured but an instant.

The horse she had been given to ride at the way station bore a Circle Cross brand. It had turned up lame earlier in the morning, Lucy explained.

"If Mark's men had seen me, I couldn't have outrun them," she admitted grimly.

Although his own roan was reasonably fresh, it would soon tire in these mountains under a double load. Unsaddling the pinto Yale turned it loose. He hid the saddle in the brush. He mounted, then helped Lucy up behind him. With her arms locked about his waist, they started away from Rafter A.

He might be able to get a fresh horse at Rafter A, but it would mean a gunfight. And she could be hurt. If something happened to him, she would truly be alone.

Because the horse would not last to the rendezvous above the Half Pine way station, Yale swung toward Rincon, which was nearer by several miles.

As they rode Yale kept scanning the countryside, looking for Rafter A men, and also for a likely place to build a fire. At last he found what he sought. A cave, barely visible through a stand of junipers. Tethering the weary roan, he set about gathering wood. He was lucky to find a few dry pieces in the cave to give the fire a start. While he worked it started raining again.

He knew to build a fire in the cave was risky, because of the smoke. But Lucy needed warmth. If the enemy located them because of the smoke he'd face up to it. Soaked, chilled to the bone, Lucy Channa could be taken with the grippe, or something worse.

When the fire blazed brightly in the cavern, he made her sit as close to it as possible. But even as the heat started to penetrate the wind changed. For a moment he thought they could weather this turn of luck; he was warming her cold hands between his own. The wind increased and the smoke blew back into the cave and they were forced to flee.

As they started riding again, he said thinly, "There's one place you can get a change of clothing. And by God she's going to help—"

He felt Lucy's arms tighten about him. "Thela would be the last person in the world to help me," Lucy said soberly.

"I'm afraid she has no choice."

"You don't know Thela."

For a moment he started somberly into the rainwashed world with funnels of sunlight beating the wet ground here and there through cracks in the overcast. The rain had tapered off again.

"I guess you're right on that point," he agreed. "I don't know Thela." With his right hand he squeezed her cold hands locked about his waist. "You have friends in Rincon? Someone who could help?"

"Not friends. Only people who used to know my family. They'd be afraid to help without letting Mark know."

"I see. Then we have no choice but to get you to Thela's."

"I don't think it's wise, Yale."

"You're going to have dry clothes and a warm place to sleep tonight. Surely all your family did for her when she was a girl will count for something."

She said nothing more. Once, from a shelf of rock above the Rincon road, they watched a buckboard and five riders sweep toward town. Because of the distance Yale could identify none of them.

He had dismounted, letting Lucy fall into his outstretched arms. As he held her close, Thela seemed a whole world away from him. They let the roan blow. It would not last many more miles. Yale prayed that it would keep going until he could sight the adobe house above Mesilla Street that he knew so well.

He mounted, then held out his hands to pull Lucy up behind him. But he lost his grip on the wet sleeve that covered one arm. With a little cry, she swung away and he almost lost his hold on her other arm. The roan, tired as it was, snorted and reared and tried to kick at the unnatural burden of the girl dangling at arm's length against a flank. Just in time Yale drew her across his lap, and managed to quiet the roan. And when this was done he found himself staring down into Lucy's face. She watched him, her blue eyes questioning. Then they softened and he bent his head. He could taste the rain on her mouth, and he felt her surge against him, murmuring his name over and over. At last they broke apart. For some distance they rode that way, Lucy sitting in his lap, face buried against his chest, hands gripping his shoulders.

With her lips against his throat, she whispered, "There should be many things to say at a time like this. I seem to be without words—"

110

"So am I. I guess I was attracted to you from the first time I saw you in Rincon. But I was too stiff-necked to admit it to myself. I had my future planned completely. Wall myself up in a private section of the world without trouble. With a hand-picked wife—"

"When you first came here I hoped you would call. But you didn't. And then I learned you were betrothed to Thela." Turning her head she peered up at him. "Do you still love her?"

Yale shook his head, and moisture from his hat brim sparkled under the brightening sun. "I'll explain to her. However, I have the feeling it won't matter too much."

CHAPTER TWENTY-ONE

Sheriff Josh Wheatley bought Duel a drink in Quincy's. Then he waved to his cronies and started for the door. Some of the steam had run out of the boys. They were not quite as fired up to ride in a posse as they had been earlier in the day. A change in weather could make a man hold off. Nobody likes to sit a wet saddle. Besides, there was plenty of time. Yale Braden wasn't about to ride off and just leave a ranch as valuable as 88.

Duel fell in step with the sheriff, adjusting his hatbrim to the sun when they stepped outside. Rain still dripped from the overhang into a fire barrel. The muddied street would begin to dry in another hour if the storm passed on.

"Thela at home?" Duel asked, slanting his yellow gaze at the older man.

"She was when I left." Wheatley, hands in his pockets, stared at the mountains rising beyond the town. "I always did favor you for a son-in-law. But then Braden came along."

"DeLong had a chance to kill him last year."

"Well, DeLong won't get another chance." Wheatley cleared his throat. "I hope you make your peace with Mark. You're entitled to a half interest in Rafter A whether Mark has a wife or not."

"Not half interest," Duel said with a cold smile, "whole interest."

"But how do you figure to—"

"That steer horn nearly did the job for me. But it's a job that'll get done."

"Surely you don't mean—"

"Mark's days have been growin' considerably shorter. Since the minute he decided not to ransom me out of that Mex prison."

When Duel turned his back and climbed jauntily toward the rundown 'dobe house at the end of the street, Sheriff Josh Wheatley felt as if small blades of ice were being sheared off into the pit of his stomach, to freeze again at a spot in his lower spine.

For Duel couldn't have said it plainer. He meant to kill his own brother.

Wheatley had taken no more than two steps when he heard the sounds of a wagon and horsemen swing in from Mesilla Street. Turning, he saw Mark Ashfork, looking pale and twenty pounds lighter. Ashfork shared the seat of a buckboard with Pop Grimsby, who was handling the team. Mark Ashfork was gripping the edge of a blanket that covered his knees. Behind Mark Ashfork were five Rafter A men, rifles across saddle pommels.

Mark Ashfork, long gray hair streaming in the wind, drew a rifle from under his blanket. Cocking it, his bellow swept the street like a high wind.

"Duel!"

Duel wheeled, started a hand for his belt, then froze. The buckboard swung in beside the plank walk, the riders strung out. Grimsby's face above the gray beard was expressionless.

For a moment the brothers stared at each other. Then Duel forced a smile. "Didn't figure to see you in town, Mark."

"What'd you do with my wife?"

"I haven't seen your wife."

"I had men hunting for her. You pulled 'em off with some fool business at Eighty-Eight—"

"It wasn't fool business, Mark—"

"I told you I was running Rafter A!" Mark Ashfork yelled, holding the rifle so rock-still on his brother that men piling into the street to savor the excitement, fully expected him to shoot. "I told you if there was gunwork to do I'd give the orders!"

"Mark, you got to understand—"

"I don't have to understand one thing you say. You black-livered bastard. And I say that in shame because of Momma and Poppa. But you're not fit to live. You had old man Peters killed."

"Now wait a minute—"

"Eph Peters rode all the way to Rafter A to tell it to me straight. That boy riskin' his neck. Not knowing whether I'd hang him or not. He said it was Rafter A men on Rafter A hosses that gunned down the old man."

"All right, I admit it," Duel said, eyeing the rifle in his brother's hands. "But I say good riddance. Everybody knows the whole hill bunch are wide-loopers—"

"And Eph also was riding to see Yale Braden to say that some of the hill crowd would side him. He seen you and your crew pull down Braden's buildings, rip up his books."

113

"Braden had it coming."

"This was all done *before* Braden fired a shot at you!"

Duel Ashfork flushed, then whitened and the rush of blood from his face seemed to pull the handsome mouth into an ugly line. His eyes sought Josh Wheatley.

"Sheriff, tell my brother that he's mistaken about Braden. Yale Braden is an outlaw and I say we oughta put a price on his head."

Mark Ashfork's grip tightened on the rifle. "Duel, I wish to hell the Mexicans had stood you against a wall and shot you full of holes!"

"I done heard enough, Mark," Duel said savagely. "If you figure to shoot me in the back, you have at it."

Duel started walking again up the slant toward the Wheatley house.

Mark shouted after him, "Every man who went on that Eighty-Eight raid is fired. Santo, Toll, the whole lot."

Duel continued climbing, not looking back. His chin strap swayed across the front of his shirt.

"And as for you," Mark shouted at his brother, "don't set foot again on Rafter A. Ever!"

When Pop Grimsby had driven Mark down to Quincy's, Wheatley filled the gap of silence. Turning to the men who had gathered along the stret, the sheriff said, "So far as most of us are concerned, Braden is still a man to hunt down whenever we figure to get at it."

"We're with you, Sheriff!" a man said.

In the saloon, Mark Ashfork moved painfully to the bar. There he leaned a moment to get his breath, while the drinkers watched in a strained silence.

"Listen to me," he said hoarsely, having spent himself in his raging against Duel. "One thousand dollars to the man who brings my wife home to Rafter A where she belongs."

A dozen of the men threw down their drinks and stormed out, eager to claim the reward. In the sudden quiet, Mark Ashfork made his way to one of the tables and sank tiredly to a chair.

In a voice he thought was loud, but which was in reality only a hoarse whisper, he ordered a bottle of whisky.

CHAPTER TWENTY-TWO

Purposely Yale left the road when he neared Rincon, and cut right to an old mining trail he remembered. On one of the few times he had ridden with Thela, they had taken this route. In light of what he now knew, how incongruous it seemed for Thela to hate horses and anything pertaining to ranch life. When once her father had earned his living as bronc-buster for the late Ron Channa.

It was a good thing, he reflected as they began the climb through the aspens, that Rincon lay just ahead. The roan, carrying double all the way from Rafter A, was just about done. Once it faltered and Yale considered the possibility that they would be afoot. But the animal managed to find another burst of strength and reached the summit of the trail, then began the descent.

Finally he could see the sprawling 'dobe house ahead through the trees. Fifty yards from the house he dismounted and tied the roan, then he helped Lucy to the ground. Cautiously they approached the house.

His knock brought an instant response. The kitchen door opened and the Camacho woman put out her dark head.

"*Que es*—" And then she saw Lucy Channa. Her plump brown face beamed as she rushed to the girl and hugged her. A spate of Spanish rolled from her lips. Lucy was finally able to break away from the old woman.

Lucy turned to Yale, her eyes wet. "Her mother worked for us when I was a little girl," she explained.

Yale was peering beyond the woman, into the house. He could see no one stirring. "Is Thela home?" he asked. When Lucy Camacho shook her head, he inquired about the sheriff. She said Josh Wheatley was downtown somewhere.

"Is no matter," she said happily to Lucy. "In this house you are always welcome. As long as I am here."

She drew them into the kitchen. The aroma of fresh-baked bread hung in the warm air. Lucy and the woman talked together for a moment, then went into another part of the house.

Yale stood beside the big stove, peering out the side win-

dow. Through his mind ran the words he would try to say
to Thela. She preferred this house to a husband, he would
say. Out on the trail it had seemed fairly easy to make her
understand how things stood between them. Then his only concern had been to get Lucy Channa to a place of safety. She
needed warmth and a change of clothing. For two nights,
she had lived like an animal in the brush, trying to elude the
searchers. She had suffered from lack of food, intermittent
rains and mud. But she was a product of this tough country
and the elements could not whip her.

The sound of a buggy at the side gate alerted him. Quickly
he moved to the window that overlooked the cracked 'dobe
wall. He saw Duel Ashfork, wearing a yellow slicker, holding in a team of matched blacks hitched to a livery stable
buggy. Thela jumped down, her mouth shaking. She turned,
her back stiff.

"At least I thought you were a gentleman," she flung at
Duel.

When he smiled his teeth were very white against his dark
face. "You're not going to have an easy time in life. If
you honestly believe any man you decide to give yourself to
figures to put a ring on your finger—"

"You try to make me out a slut!"

"It was your idea to get out of the rain in Rafferty's barn,
not mine."

Thela reacted as if he had slapped her. And, as was her
habit, she abruptly changed tactics. She held out a hand to
him.

"Duel, I shouldn't have lost my temper, but— We've known
each other so long, and—"

"I've got other plans when it comes to marriage. I figure
when the time comes, to marry with Mark's widow!"

"Lucinda Channa? You wouldn't dare do that to me! You
wouldn't *dare*!"

But Duel was driving off down the hill, laughing.

Thela stormed into the house. She came to a halt when
she saw Yale there beside the kitchen windows. And as her
eyes raked his face, knowledge that he had overheard the
exchange with Duel burst upon her. But before she could
say anything Lucy and the Camacho woman came in from
another part of the house.

Lucy said, "Thela, I needed help and there was nowhere
else to go—"

Thela was staring at her. Lucy wore a pale green dress.

Much too short for she had more height than Thela. Slowly Thela's face went white.

"My dress! You're wearing *my* dress!"

The Camacho woman looked disgusted and started to say something. For one startled moment Yale thought Thela would fling herself at Lucy and try to claw the girl's face. Instead, she whirled out of the house, her skirts flying.

He saw her rush down the hill. Her hair coming unpinned. "Yale Braden!" she cried, pointing back toward the house. "Yale Braden!"

Already she had attracted the attention of a knot of men in front of the gun shop run by the late Jake Byerly. Drawing guns, they started for the house. Others joined them.

Grabbing Lucy by the wrist Yale pulled her into the rear yard. He had nearly reached the roan when he spotted a yellow slicker in the trees. Duel Ashfork had evidently heard Thela's screams and swung the buggy team back to the house. Now he was coming afoot, gripping a revolver.

"My lucky day!" he cried; there was more turmoil in the street, men shouting, pouring up into the trees.

Yale gave Lucy a shove, drew his gun. Before he could fire, two men leaped upon his back. As he tried to turn and fling them off, a third hit him a stunning blow in the face.

Their combined weight drove him face down into the mud. He remembered Lucy screaming his name. Then cold steel clamped hard against his wrists.

Sheriff Josh Wheatley straightened up, and looked around at the crowd. "That'll hold him."

Yale was jerked to his feet. The yard swarmed with hard-eyed men.

Duel gave Yale a tight smile, then turned to the sheriff. "Josh, you like to talk big about savin' money for the county. Anybody got a rope?"

Wheatley avoided Yale's eyes. He stood rigid in a shaft of sunlight that broke through the trees. "Duel, this is some different than running a man down with a posse. This is right in town."

"No difference," Duel snarled.

As a clamor went up from the crowd, a rope snaked over the stout limb of a tree near the gate. For a moment Wheatley stared at it, then he said, "I won't let you do a thing like this." And Yale had a fleeting moment of hope, that Josh Wheatley had become his own man at last.

But that hope crumbled when Wheatley went on, "My

117

daughter figures to spend her life in this house. I won't blight it by letting you hang a man in the back yard."

Duel, staring at the sheriff a moment, holstered his revolver. "All right, Josh, I'll give in. We'll take him downtown. The livery barn has stout rafters."

Yale stood in the grip of half a dozen men, hands manacled behind his back. The blow to his face had partially stunned him. He could hear a vast roaring in his ears. He caught a distorted vision of Lucy, wearing Thela's too-tight dress, trying to fight her way to his side. During their brief interlude in the Wheatley house Lucy had borrowed a comb from the Camacho woman to get the tangles out of her hair. But it had come unpinned, to spill about her face.

For a moment he stared at her numbly, then his vision cleared. Men were arguing, gesturing wildly.

"Lucy!" Yale cried above the tumult. "Get out of here!"

Somehow his voice seemed to bring her to the crowd's attention for the first time. A man sprang for her, and another. A fight broke out between the pair.

One of them cried, "I seen her first!"

"It was me, dammit. My thousand dollars!"

With a desperate lunge, Yale tried to reach her side, but was hauled back, a man dragging on each arm.

Duel was staring at Lucy amusedly. "That's right, my brother did offer a thousand dollars for her hide." He gestured at Yale Braden. "Forget the woman. Let's get Braden to the livery and get shut of him."

The suggestion was greeted with another shout of agreement. However, those concerned with the reward for Mark Ashfork's wife were still disputing prior claims bitterly. Others had joined in.

As Yale was marched down the street, he could hear Thela sobbing in the big empty house she demanded as part of her life. And in that moment, with hands gripping his arms, enveloped by the blood heat of these men who sought to kill him, Yale wondered who would go to Thela now. Who would stroke her sleek head and murmur, "Don't cry. Don't cry."

CHAPTER TWENTY-THREE

Mark Ashfork slumped in a chair at one of the deserted deal tables in Quincy's Saloon. Glumly he stared at the coating of fresh sawdust on the floor, smelling stale beer, and old wood and leather. The only other occupant at the table was Pop Grimsby, who cradled his shotgun across the lap that was usually covered by a flour sack apron. There was only a sprinkling of drinkers at the bar. The shouts from the upper part of town had drawn everyone else.

A fat man observed, "Hangings always turn my stomach. Can't eat for a week after I see one."

Mark Ashfork looked up. "Who they figure to hang, Pop?"

The gray-haired old cook shifted the shotgun on his lap, but made no reply. And Mark gave a snort of disgust, aimed at himself for always forgetting that for ten years or more Pop Grimsby couldn't have heard a full barrel dropped off the roof of the Gadsen House, with him standing two feet away.

Mark Ashfork had his question answered by someone else. A man thrust his head over the doors and said excitedly, "They've caught Yale Braden."

The pronouncement did not cause Mark to even look around at the man in the doorway. The ride to town in the buckboard had sapped his strength. Grimsby got up and went to the bar and signaled the bartender for a beer. He stood there, hat cuffed back on his gray head, drinking from the bottle. Some of the brew spilled into his beard.

There was more distant shouting now, a gunshot. Mark felt of his chest. His wound had started to throb again and his mouth tasted of fever. He knew full well what had caused his setback. It was the fact that this girl he had married, to whom he had promised so much; this girl who wanted only to be his widow, not his wife—loathed him.

Outside the shouting was closer now. He could hear the tramp of boots. Then the swinging doors burst open and he saw this woman whose scornful eyes would haunt him to his grave.

She stood there, this Lucy Channa, staring at him. No, by

God, he corrected himself. She was Mrs. Mark Ashfork, according to the laws of the Territory of New Mexico. Foot by foot she was shoved forward by the men who flanked her.

"I claim the reward, Mark," shouted one.

"No. I'm the one who saw her—"

Mark Ashfork got slowly to his feet, and somehow the sight of his craggy face twisted in rage, silenced the men. He put out a hand to the back of a chair to steady his trembling legs. With the other hand he drew his revolver.

"Stand aside!" he cried. "Who brings my wife into a saloon? A place where no respectable woman ever walks."

Following this outburst, only one of them had the nerve to speak up. "But, Mark, we only claim the reward—" The rest were backing toward the doors, ready to burst for the street.

Taking a deep breath, Mark Ashfork holstered the revolver. He straightened up, as far as the wound would allow. Slowly he walked toward his bride, a towering gray-thatched figure in rough range clothes. He must not show any weakness in her eyes. She must think him strong. He was strong.

"I must speak with you," she said, her voice, low, controlled. Her eyes stared, unwavering. Only the whiteness at her lips betrayed an inner agitation.

Putting out his arm to her, he said, "We'll go to my room at the Gadsen House."

Without hesitation she took his arm and walked out of the saloon with him. Those who had hustled her down the hill to claim the reward, made no move to press their claims.

Pop Grimsby, shotgun under his arm, trailed the bride and groom ten places behind, up the steep walk.

The rancher and his bride climbed the veranda steps of the hotel. Lucy in a tight green dress, too short, showing her ankles. He started to lead her into the hotel, but she drew back and walked to a far corner of the veranda. The shouting, the loud voices had started up again, and were drawing closer.

Mark cocked his ear at the sounds for a moment, then shot her an ugly glance. "You're here because of Braden," he accused.

"Yes."

Some men had come out of the hotel to stare. Mark turned on them, some of the old familiar bellow back in his voice. "Clear out, the lot of you!" And they cleared mighty sudden.

Then Mark added in a milder tone, "A man wants words

120

with his own wife. In private." He scowled at Lucy. "You did not come to me of your own free will. They forced you."

"I will make a bargain."

"What bargain is there!" he cried. "You're my wife. That's the bargain you made."

"Listen to me—"

"My money in exchange for the privilege of putting a ring on your finger."

The noisy crowd was drawing closer, and she desperately tried to make him understand. "You know I don't want your money. I thought you were dying—" Her face lost color. A burst of voices came from the alley behind the hotel. The sounds of men in a hurry.

"You know they intend killing Yale Braden," she said.

"It's none of my affair," he said thinly, and leaned against the veranda rail to ease the strain on his tired legs.

Men poured into the livery stable down the block. Others joined them until Mesilla Street was nearly deserted. Horsemen, drawn by the excitement, pounded in from all directions. Mothers screamed at children and dogs made their own brand of noise.

Again Lucy tried to get Mark to understand. But he stubbornly glared at her. Suddenly she moved to his side. Before his dulled reflexes reacted she had drawn his holstered revolver. Lifting the weapon with both hands, she placed the barrel at her temple. Her mouth was white, her eyes mirroring shock.

As he stared in amazement, she said, "I loathe the person who would take his own life. But if Yale Braden hangs, I will trip the hammer of this gun. And you will have no bride."

Mark Ashfork's gaze instantly brightened. "And if he don't hang?"

"I come to you willingly."

A sudden savage smile burst at the corners of his mouth, then hardened. "You've been out all this time with Braden. They catched you together."

"I rode some distance with him, yes."

"I tell you this." His voice trembled. "I claimed you as my virgin bride. If you prove to be otherwise, I'll hunt Braden down. And I'll put the 'Paches to shame with the sort of death he'll have."

She looked him in the eye. "You don't need to worry."

"All right. I tell you this. I will be fair. He won't hang, if

121

I can help it. Now give me the gun." He held out his hand. She hesitated a moment then gave him the revolver.

Mark Ashfork looked around for Pop Grimsby, but the old man was gone. Digging a key from his pocket, Mark said, "Go to my room and lock yourself in. Wait for me."

"I think I'd better go with you. To make sure the promise is kept."

Returning the key to his pocket, he hurried her down the walk toward the livery stable. They were twenty feet from the wide doors of the building when there was a sudden "Ahhhhhhh——" that burst from the assemblage.

Lucy's knees buckled and she would have fallen had not Mark Ashfork flung an arm about her waist. "They've killed him," she sobbed.

Mark's eyes darkened. "Goddam Duel, if we're too late I'll shoot that brother of mine." He literally dragged Lucy to the entrance, tearing men aside with his free hand. He glimpsed the rope slung over a rafter. But there was no tension on it, as would be the case if it supported a body.

Then he knew the reason for the exclamation that had made him certain Yale Braden was hanged. It was because Pop Grimsby had slipped behind Duel and was holding the muzzles of a cocked shotgun against his back. Duel stood, as if carved from a shaft of dark stone, hands wide from his belt. The crowd watched, no one daring to make a move because of the murderous hair-trigger shotgun that could blow Duel to pieces.

Three feet from Duel, Yale Braden stood with a noose about his neck. His face was white, but his eye was steady. And seeing that Yale still lived, Lucy Channa found the strength to stand on her own feet instead of collapsing against her husband for support.

Duel swung his yellow gaze at Mark. "Get this hellion off my back."

But Mark ignored his brother. He was looking at the gray-bearded Rafter A cook who had been known as Tex in his younger years.

"I'll be damned," Mark breathed. "You ain't as deaf as you let on. You overheard me say I didn't want Braden hanged."

Pop Grimsby, holding the shotgun, nodded. "That's right. I come down here to give you a little more time. I figured Duel would want to get it over fast."

"Thanks, Pop. But I don't figure why all these years you played deaf."

"Because when I got old I wasn't no good shootin' a gun no more. I figured if your riders thought I was deaf, they'd be a little careless when they talked around me. I never trusted Duel none."

Duel looked back over his shoulder at Grimsby. "Old man, you're through at Rafter A."

Mark's voice thundered across the crowded stable. "You don't own that ranch, I do."

"We'll see," Duel said under his breath.

Mark Ashfork strode up and flung the noose from Braden's neck. When he saw that the rancher's wrists were manacled, he looked around the mass of faces. "Where the hell's Josh Wheatley?" he demanded.

"He's out back," a man offered.

"Get him in here."

An aisle formed from the wagon yard, and Wheatley came up, trying to smile. "Mark, I figured you'd want him hanged, so—"

"Unlock them handcuffs!"

Wheatley did as he was told. Then Yale Braden was rubbing his wrists. Pop Grimsby stepped away from Duel, letting down the hammers of his shotgun.

"Spread the word!" Mark Ashfork boomed at the crowd. "As far south as Paso Del Norte. I'm paying double wages to men with guts who're not afraid to shoot a gun." Then his gaze centered on his younger brother. "If it's war you want, that's what you'll get!"

Duel took a tug at his belt. He glared at Lucy who had come to stand beside Mark Ashfork. "One of these days," he snarled at the girl, "you'll crawl on your knees through *cholla* if I tell you to."

With an angry shout, Yale Braden started for Duel. But Mark inserted his bulk between the two men. "I'll handle the insults to my wife, if you don't mind, Braden."

Yale stepped back, his face tight with anger. Duel was stomping out of the livery barn.

Mark Ashfork looked around. "Free whisky for the lot of you!" he bellowed at the crowd. "Tell Quincy you're to have all you can hold for the rest of the day. Compliments of Rafter A."

Shouting, the men crowded for the exits.

Yale was staring at Lucy who stood awkwardly at Mark Ashfork's side, eyes downcast.

Mark said, "Braden, I'm givin' you this one chance to get out of the country. Go down to Paso Del Norte. Wait

123

there. As soon as I can arrange to transfer funds, you'll have twenty thousand dollars for your Eighty-Eight. You'll also have your neck. Don't never come back to New Mexico."

Yale saw Lucy slowly lift her head and look at him. Deliberately she raised her hand to let it rest on Mark Ashfork's arm.

She said, "I fought for a long time. But at last I know my place. It is with my husband."

"This is your own decision?" he asked her quietly.

"It is."

"Then I guess there's nothing further for me to say."

But as Yale started away, Mark Ashfork said, "Where are your men, Braden?"

Yale looked around. "They've drifted."

"I don't figure to have them trying to stir up trouble after you've gone."

"Striker and some of the others have wanted to go back to Texas for a long time." Yale kept his features straight feeling no guilt because circumstances forced him to lie.

"If you run into any of them drifters," Mark said thinly, "you give 'em the same message I give you. They're to stay outa New Mexico."

"I understand."

"There's a southbound due shortly," Mark said. "You be on that stage. Don't get off till Paso Del Norte."

Yale nodded that he understood. He looked around this cavernous structure with its odors of horse sweat and hay. A few short minutes ago a pack of men had decided that he was to die here. And this would have happened had it not been for the sudden appearance of the Rafter A cook with his shotgun coming up unnoticed behind Duel in the swirling crowd.

He went to the walk and stared at the clear sky. Later a black depression settled over him when he saw Lucy Channa ride out with Mark in the Rafter A buckboard. Six riders, including Pop Grimsby aboard a livery stable saddler, trailed them.

He had no money, no gun. And he needed a mount. He looked carefully around when the Rafter A cavalcade had disappeared. Men were eying him.

Trying to appear casual, he turned back into the stable. He had to move carefully, because with Mark out of town there would be enough hotheads left who might finish their business with the rope. If he provoked them.

124

CHAPTER TWENTY-FOUR

Yale had taken no more than half a dozen steps when Josh Wheatley called to him. Yale turned, swearing under his breath at the delay. He needed to get his hands on a gun, and fast. He needed a horse and here was the sheriff wearing his politician's smile.

"Mark told me to make arrangements for your ticket," Wheatley said. "Your passage is paid all the way to Paso."

"Much thanks," Yale snapped.

"Now, Yale, I know how you feel." The sheriff looked apologetic. "You got to see how things are—"

"Never mind telling me. I understand. It all depends on which way the wind blows. One time it blows for me. One time it blows toward Duel. But now it's blowing toward Mark again."

"Afraid you don't understand at all, son." Wheatley thumbed his mustache. "I think you and Thela could be mighty happy. With that twenty thousand Mark pays for your ranch, you could go to California like you planned. And I could come out and visit you in a year or so."

"I think not, Josh. I think definitely not."

Josh Wheatley slowly reddened. Deliberately he turned on his heel and swung up the walk toward Quincy's where most of the male inhabitants of Rincon were lapping up Rafter A whisky.

Yale swallowed. His throat was dry. He longed mightily for a shot of that liquid Quincy was so freely dispensing. But there was no use wishing for the impossible. He would be satisfied if he could find a gun in the stable office. And with any luck at all locate a saddled horse out back.

As he angled for the cubicle in the shadows that passed for an office, he heard a stirring. For the first time he saw four armed men regarding him from the shelter of a hay pile.

"Get back on the street," one of them said. "Mark give us orders to see you get on that stage."

"If you don't," another put in, "you're a dead man, Braden."

Without a word Yale turned and went to stand in front

of the Gadsen House where the southbound would pull in. The four men kept watching him.

And when the stage rolled in with a popping of leathers, a rattle of wheels, Yale swung aboard. The other passengers were drummers and a slender man going over mining reports.

Sheriff Wheatley was saying something to the driver. Then he came and put his face at the coach window. "If I hadn't given my word to Mark to see you safely out of town, I'd let the boys finish you with a rope."

"I've done nothing to you, Josh," Yale said stiffly, as the three passengers looked on.

"You broke Thela's heart," Josh Wheatley said coldly. "I'll never forgive you for that."

Before Yale could answer the stage wheeled away from the walk.

And then as the stage gained momentum on the downgrade, one of the Rafter A men came pounding into town. The rider shouted to those in front of the saloon.

"Anybody seen the Reverend Burkhalter! I got to fetch him. Mark figures to marry the Channa girl all over again!"

Yale heard only part of it, because of the noisy stage, the pound of the team on the muddy street.

The passengers were eying him, but only the one with the mining reports spoke. "Run out of town on a rail?"

"So to speak," Yale said. They were out of town now, onto the road that snaked down the mountain. The sky was clearing, but whenever they passed under an archway of trees, drops of moisture made buckshot sounds on the stage roof.

Some miles south of town Yale leaned out the window and shouted up at the driver. "Stop at Half Pine!"

"No stop on the southbound 'less there's passengers to pick up."

"I have a message to pass on from Mark Ashfork. Something I have to tell Olcutt!"

"Well, I dunno—"

"Listen to me, you fool" Yale cried above the wind, the slog of hooves in the mud. "It's Rafter A business!"

When the Half Pine station came into view, Olcutt was out front to wave the stage on. But the driver slowed enough for Yale to jump off. He lit, running, almost lost his balance, then righted himself. Olcutt stared at him warily, then started backing toward the way station.

The stage had finally halted down the road. The driver, holding in the team, twisted around on the high seat to stare at Yale.

"Your passage is paid to Paso. You figure to ride on with us?"

"No!"

"But the sheriff said—"

Yale motioned for him to go on and in a moment the stage swung out of sight around a bend in the tree-lined road.

Olcutt had tried to duck inside the station, but Yale caught him by an arm and pushed him against the wall.

"My men," he said tensely. "Are they still around?"

Olcutt shook his head. "Right after you left that herd of Mex cows come through."

"Duel's herd?"

"Yep. 'Bout fifteen Mexes pushin' 'em. They crossed the road about a mile south. Your men figured Duel ordered his crew to spread that herd on your land, Braden."

Yale dropped his hand from Olcutts' arm, swearing softly under his breath. He knew that Striker and the rest of the crew would likely get themselves slaughtered, trying to prevent Duel's *vaqueros* from reaching 88 with the herd.

"I'll need a fresh horse," Yale told the way station operator.

Olcutt's fat face lost a little color. "But if Rafter A hears I helped you—"

"I'll also need a revolver and some shells. And quit fretting. When this is over maybe there won't be any Rafter A for you to worry about."

But Yale knew he was talking the big wind. He was only a puny man with a bent sword, facing up to the might of an enraged grizzly.

On a bay horse, a pistol at his belt, Yale rode out, north through the pass. Within a mile he came across the tracks of cattle. Risking discovery he climbed to a ridge where he could make better time. He needed his men desperately. He had to save Lucy Channa. A herd of Mex cows on his grass was not nearly as important. For he knew full well that Lucy had made a bargain; the neck of one Yale Braden in exchange for the bed and board of Mark Ashfork.

He pushed the bay unmercifully. Clouds gathered, spilled rain. Thunder rolled against the higher peaks and lightning sent a great tree crashing.

At last he saw the herd far below, a great mass of horns and hide. But he saw no sign of his own men. He rode a few miles ahead, then descended to the wreckage of his buildings, staying far enough back so as not to be trapped if Duel had left guards. He studied the ground. No fresh sign. If his riders had come this way at all they had been mounted on winged horses.

He hoped to pick up a fresh mount, but his corrals were empty. Another score to settle with Rafter A.

Despondently he turned the bay for a higher trail that would allow him to reach the distant Rafter A headquarters without going through town.

CHAPTER TWENTY-FIVE

The rider Mark Ashfork had sent to town had two orders to carry out. In addition to rounding up the Reverend Burkhalter, the man was ordered to bring back to Rafter A a white dress of some sort that would fit Lucy Channa. At Mrs. Goodenough's dressmaking establishment something could be found, Mark was certain. Perhaps a dress being made for one of the other ladies of Rincon. And Mark was sure the woman, whoever she might be, wouldn't mind giving up the dress for such an occasion. And even if she objected, her husband would be an adequate persuader when he learned that it was a special request from the owner of the powerful Rafter A.

Within the hour the Reverend Burkhalter, looking more harrassed than usual, rode out with the Rafter A man in a rented wagon. The reverend carried over his arm a white dress, protected from the elements by a clean blanket. The dress and blanket had come from Mrs. Goodenough herself. It was her own wedding gown. She was a tall widow and it was certain the dress would be a proper fit for the younger woman.

Later, Lucy Channa woodenly entered the main house at Rafter A. The structure sprawled across the end of the shelf of land where the headquarters buildings were located. It was of log and stone, with huge fireplaces and windows so narrow they allowed little light to enter the cheerless place.

In the hall Mark caught Lucy by the arms, and peered down at her sternly. "We're doin' it right this time, Lucy. This time you're wearin' a proper dress. This time you're goin' to smile at your husband. This time you're goin' to let me put the ring on your finger. This time you're goin' to leave it there. This time when Burkhalter says we're man an' wife, you're goin' to turn your face to me. And you're goin' to kiss your husband like a bride should. Do you understand?"

"I understand." She put a hand to her forehead. "May I go to my room while we wait for the reverend?"

"You can go to our room. You wait there till I send for

129

you." He put a hand on her shoulder, his voice softening. "I want everything to be done proper this time."

He led her along a corridor littered with catch ropes and saddles and boots. On both walls rifles hung from pegs. He opened a door and told her to go in and wait. He stepped back out of the room and closed the door.

For a moment she stood woodenly, then she dropped to her knees, and tears spilled across the front of her dress.

Later, when she heard a wagon in the yard, she thought the moment had come. But then the voices of her aunt and uncle reached her from the parlor.

Slowly she got to her feet and looked at the big bed that seemed to overflow the room. In the center of the headboard was a Rafter A brand. The room smelled of tobacco and old boots. She walked to a window. It was narrow, little more than a rifle slot. Too small for escape, even if she considered it. She had given her word and she meant to keep it.

Finally her aunt, beaming, stepped into the room. She crossed swiftly to her niece, searching her face.

"Lucy, don't be so downcast."

"How can I help it?" Lucy rubbed her arms.

"I know what bothers you. But it can't be helped. It's why we're women." And when Lucy continued to stare out the side window, her aunt went on, "But it's your duty as a wife. No woman likes it, but—"

"You don't have to explain," Lucy said crisply. "I was brought up on a ranch. Don't you think I know about these things? All I had to do was keep my eyes open."

"I'm so glad." Her aunt was dabbing at moist cheeks. "I thought maybe you didn't know about the demands a husband would make—"

"Stop it, Aunt Martha, please."

"We're so happy for you. Pete and me. So happy that you've come to your senses."

"Senses? If I'd had any at all, I'd have left this country when my father was killed."

Her aunt, recovered from the tears-for-joy moment, said, "The wedding's to be held soon as the reverend gets here. You know what? Mark's promised to send me and Pete on a trip to Frisco. Won't that be grand?"

"Grand," the girl said dully.

"Can't you at least be happy for us, child?" Her aunt sounded aggrieved. "After all, we've had some terrible years. My brother was killed and—"

130

"Your brother, maybe. But he was my father. And you expect me to be blushingly girlish when I go to this man who ordered my father's death."

"But Mark said you promised—"

"So I did. I intend to keep it."

Her aunt suddenly sat up straighter on the bed. "And what happens after that?"

"Who knows."

"You're not going to do something—crazy. I remember what you said. That if you were ever forced—well, to really be Mark's wife, that you—"

"For once why don't you allow me to manage my own affairs?"

Out front, in the parlor, Pete Hatcher was drinking Mark Ashfork's whisky, one leg slung over the end of a sofa. He was discussing the beef market as if, along with a rich husband for his niece, he had suddenly acquired a vast knowledge of cows and drover's costs and the exhorbitant rates one paid at Abilene—

Mark Ashfork barely heard him. To celebrate the occasion he tried to smoke a cigar. But he found that trying to draw the smoke into his lungs made his chest pain. The hours had dragged by and he began to wonder if maybe he wasn't a fool. He was married already, why go through it a second time? Take his rights now, by God. But then he knew he had to bring that girl to harness. This time she would go through with the ceremony, giving him the respect owed a husband. In due time he would show her that he had started to make amends for some of the black deeds of his life.

Hatcher's reedy voice was getting on his nerves. Lucinda Channa's uncle acted like a man who suddenly discovered that the lumps in his stony yard were in reality deposits of pure gold.

Mark Ashfork glanced at a corner clock. Where in the hell was the Reverend Burkhalter? He should have been here before this.

When he tried to draw on the cigar again the pain increased in his chest.

"Goin' to the bunkhouse and send some boys to town," Mark said over his shoulder.

It was full dark in the yard now. Bunkhouse windows blazed with light. Wearily he made his way across the rutted yard. The one concession he had made to Duel, was to allow the wounded to stay here. The others who had participated in the

131

raid on Yale Braden's 88 were fired. The dead were buried out back of the barn.

Before Mark reached the end of the yard his legs almost gave out. He had to pause for breath. At last he was able to continue, his breathing hard now.

When he came to stand in the bunkhouse doorway it seemed incongruous that the place wasn't swarming with men. He could see the wounded in the bunks, some of them staring at him.

At the big table five hands, playing poker, interrupted their game to watch him, waiting for orders.

In the old days, Mark thought, there should have been thirty men in the bunkhouse. He had these five hands left here at the home ranch. And there were five more out in the hills at the scattered Rafter A line shacks. Any day now men would start drifting in, anxious to earn the double wages he had announced in Rincon. He'd have a crew that could kick Duel out of New Mexico, if it came to that.

"You boys saddle up," Mark told his men. "Hit the town road. When you run into the reverend, put him on the fastest hoss you got and bring him here."

The men scrambled to do his bidding. When they had ridden out, pounding along the Rincon road, Mark staggered over to the cookshack.

Pop Grimsby sat in a tipped-back chair, feet on a meat block. On a narrow table was his shotgun.

Mark managed a savage grin. "Hello, you deaf old hellion you."

Grimsby smiled through the wiry gray beard. Then he stared soberly. "I owed your folks a lot. They took me in when—Well, never mind. What I done was my way of payin' you back. I knew if I kept my mouth shut and my ears open I'd be able to tell you things you oughta know."

"For one thing you let me know it was Duel stealing from his own brother." Mark's mouth hardened at the memory. "And not Ron Channa rustling my cows."

"You shouldn't have sent all your boys to town, Mark. Duel might—"

"Duel's got that Mex herd to worry about. He knows better than to set foot on Rafter A again." Mark turned for the door. "I want you up to the big house for the wedding."

When had had gone, Pop Grimsley shook his head slowly from side to side. Mark looked poorly. He looked real poorly tonight. Mark was hard-pressed by all that had happened. The way that Lucy Channa had scorned him had hurt Mark.

It had done something to his pride and Mark was out to make her look up to him, one way or another.

He wondered how it would be having a woman at the big house after all these years. It would be mighty strange, no denying that.

Stepping to the cookshack door Pop peered down the long shadowy yard, to see if Mark had made it back to the big house all right. But he saw no sign of movement and guessed Mark was still strong enough to navigate.

He set the coffee pot on a stove lid to heat. He hated it that Mark wanted him there for the wedding. Why didn't Mark just go ahead and take what was his by rights, and to hell with it? Why go through the whole thing over again. But Mark was stubborn. He had his own way of doing things and by God that was the way it was done.

A sound caused him to turn from the big stove. Duel Ashfork stood in the doorway. Lamplight touched the yellow eyes. Pop Grimsby noticed that Duel held his right hand out of sight, behind him. A dark fear licked through the old man as he froze there by the stove. Carefully he set down the cup he was going to use for his coffee. He moved the pot off the stove, trying not to alarm Duel unnecessarily. Duel had not spoken a word, just stood there with that crooked grin on his handsome face.

Then as Pop turned from the stove he saw at the window the faces of Charlie Santo and Eddie Toll.

Desperately he lunged for the shotgun, but he never made it. Duel stepped in close, his right hand appearing. Steel glinted in the lamplight. Pop Grimsby coughed and fell back upon a chair, splintering it.

As he lay there, the shaft of steel in his chest, Duel unloaded the shotgun and flung shells and weapon far across the yard in the shadows.

Then the three men were gone, moving quietly toward the big house.

CHAPTER TWENTY-SIX

Out of Rincon Yale Braden hit the Rafter A road. With the night wind tearing at his eyes he thought of how much this day had brought. Through these very hills he had ridden with Lucy. And now she was a virtual prisoner at Rafter A, a fact that he meant to remedy. He had no plans, but he did have a gun.

The bay horse faltered and Yale felt a drop of cold sweat roll down his side. The horse had to keep going. It *had* to. But the mount was tiring, no doubt of that. It had been a long climb over the mountains to 88, and then the wide mountainous swing around Rincon to this Rafter A road.

He rode warily, coat unbuttoned, so that any moment he could grab the weapon at his waistband. The moon was up and the wind had cleared the sky of storm clouds. The world smelled fresh and good. He wondered then why it was that men like the Ashforks had to find room on the earth, to murder and corrupt.

It seemed he had been riding for hours when suddenly he swung around a bend in the road. Abruptly he came upon a wagon sideways in the road. The right front wheel had crumpled against an outcropping of granite. Obviously the driver had been pushing the team, and tried to made the turn too fast. The vehicle had skidded in the mud. The team stood a few yards away. A cowhand, face shadowed by the brim of a big hat was trying to unhitch one of the horses, obviously to use as a saddler. Sitting in the center of the road, probably dazed when flung from the wagon, was the Reverend Burkhalter. Across his lap was a muddied white dress.

Yale had come upon them so suddenly that both men just stared. And likely the team had been snorting and prancing, still spooked by the accident, so that the sounds they made covered his approach.

The cowhand recovered from his surprise, dropped the knife he had been using to cut harness. He reached for his gun.

Yale had hauled in the bay and now he shouted, "Don't

134

try it!" and his own revolver was pointed squarely at the cowhand. The man slowly lifted his hands.

The Reverend Burkhalter struggled to his feet. "Braden, you'll help us. Mark will be furious. I don't know what he'll say about this ruined dress—"

Yale, resting his cocked revolver on the saddlehorn said, "Get his gun, Reverend. I don't aim to have him try to shoot me in the back when I ride off."

The Rafter A man sputtered and threatened, and the reverend added his own dire predictions as to Yale Braden's fate if he interfered with this wedding. But at last Burkhalter did as Yale ordered and handed up, butt first, the gun he had taken from the Rafter A hand. Shoving the extra weapon in his belt, Yale rode close to the wagon, made sure there was no rifle under the seat, then spurred the bay down the road.

Again the bay broke its stride, then pounded on. Yale licked his lips. Of late he seemed to be running out of horse flesh. This was rough country for a mount.

As he approached Rafter A he knew it would be prudent to get off the road, so he would minimize any chance of being seen by the enemy. But fighting a trail through the brush at night would slow him considerably. Dangerous as it might be he could make much better time by keeping to the road. And he'd risked his neck already, that much was for sure.

A few miles from Rafter A he suddenly heard the rattle of hoofbeats. Slowing the bay, he listened. Riders coming his way along the road. Coming fast. Almost upon him.

Reining in he desperately looked for a place to hide. He had been cutting through a long canyon, and at first glance there seemed to be nothing but sheer rock walls rising from both sides of the trail. Then as the thunder of hoofbeats seemed about to engulf him he spotted a defile, angling off to his right. Quickly he swung the bay into the sanctuary. He dismounted swiftly and clapped a hand over the animal's nostrils so it wouldn't give him away.

The riders were in the canyon now, touched by a shaft of moonlight. Bent over saddlehorns, hatbrims peeled back by the wind. Heading in the direction of Rincon. He didn't stop to ponder the reason for the hard gallop this time of night. If they were Rafter A men, which was reasonable to suppose, they would soon come upon the Reverend Burkhalter and the cowhand Yale had disarmed. They would soon come upon the Reverend Burkhalter and the cowhand

Yale had disarmed. They would be after him, that was for sure. However, this was in the future. And he took small consolation in the fact that if they were Rafter A men, there would be five less for him to deal with when he reached the ranch. He started riding again.

Finally he saw the ranch buildings with narrow yellow strips of lamplighted windows against the night. Now the road climbed abruptly. He had never been this close before. Drawing one of the revolvers he felt the butt cold in his hand. Tensely he slowed, peering ahead. Any guard there at the main gate might think a lone rider to be Rafter A. And not realize his mistake until too late.

When he passed through the open gate no one challenged him. He kept the bay at a walk. The horse was breathing hard, throwing foam. Deliberately Yale kept to the deeper shadows of a barn. He could see that the bunkhouse door was ajar. He could hear a man moaning in pain. And the thought came to him that perhaps the bunkhouse held the survivors of the battle on the Rincon road above 88. Perhaps men he had shot himself—

And briefly his mind touched on his plans to be a man of peace. So taut were his nerves that he had an urge to burst out laughing. But it was not a time for laughter. It was a time for death. It was all around; another man groaned from the bunkhouse as Yale dismounted in the shadows.

CHAPTER TWENTY-SEVEN

Pete Hatcher was getting drunk. And the more he drank the larger became his plans for a cattle empire, using the Ashfork money of course. Mark tried to smoke another cigar, but the pain was more intense. He knew it was agitation, anger that rode him tonight. The hand he had sent to town for the reverend and a wedding dress was likely bellied up to the bar in Quincy's, drinking whisky. Men today had no sense of responsibility. It was some different, Mark thought bitterly, when he had been a boy back in Texas.

Again he tried to draw on the cigar, but the pain increased. Slowly he moved to the front door, trying to make out as if his legs weren't shaking. And he sensed that Hatcher watched him narrowly.

Just before he reached the door to hurl the cigar outside, the latch rattled. And he felt a shaft of rage; who in hell was trying to open his front door without bothering to knock?

He took the last faltering step. He jerked the door open, hoping he had enough breath left to bellow at the intruder. His oath was cut off short when he saw Pop Grimsby sagged against the door frame. The old cook's face seemed white as his beard.

"What's the matter with you, Pop—" And then Mark Ashfork's gaze lowered to the hilt of a knife that protruded from the cook's chest. Grimsby's knees caved. He crumpled across the threshold. With his dying gasp he muttered a name:

"Duel—"

Alarmed, Mark peered out into the shadowed yard. He saw no one. Then he stooped, trying to move the body. But he lacked the strength. Slowly he straightened up. Pete Hatcher was on his feet, his face white, staring at Grimsby's body.

"Hatcher, gimme a hand," Mark Ashfork wheezed. "We got to move him. I can't close the door with him there!"

Mark, sweating, peered out the door, trying to spot movement. Again he yelled for Hatcher to help him. And at last the man seemed to unfreeze.

But as he sprang to grab Grimsby by an ankle and haul him into the house, a gun errupted from the hall. Hatcher's legs went out from under him. As he fell he uttered a soft sad cry.

Numbly Mark pushed a hand toward his belt, then remembered he'd taken off his gunrig earlier, while he awaited the arrival of the Reverend Burkhalter. The holstered weapon lay on a chair across the room.

He saw Duel loom in the corridor, a thread of smoke drifting from the muzzle of the revolver he gripped. Crowding up behind Duel were Charlie Santo and Eddie Toll.

Mark glared at his brother. "I told you never to set foot again on Rafter A."

Duel showed his teeth, looking from Pete Hatcher, crumpled on his side, to Grimsby in the doorway. He lifted his eyes to Mark. "Just because you said stay away, you figured I would, huh?"

"I won't have you defy me!"

"I used to be scared of you, Mark, when I was a kid. I ain't scared now. I've hated you for more years than I can count."

Mark Ashfork shifted his gaze to Santo and the red-bearded Toll. "I order you out of this house!" The two men made no move to leave. Mark turned on his brother. "I'm giving you one minute to get off this ranch!"

Mark thought he was putting all the old time power into his voice. But it was only a whisper of the bellow that used to make men turn white.

Duel came deeper into the parlor. He nodded at the dead cook. "I figured I shut him up for good. But guess he'd walk to hell and back with a knife in his gut to warn you."

For the first time in his life Mark was bewildered. He had given an order and it was refused. His own brother had expressed intense hatred for him. He took a step toward Duel, then halted. Needles of pain ripped through his chest. He realized then that a woman had been screaming since the roar of the gunshot had shaken the house. It was Martha Hatcher.

Farther back in the hall, behind Charlie Santo and Toll, he saw his wife. She stood, rigid with shock, hand pressed to her mouth as she stared at her uncle sprawled on the floor near Grimsby's body.

And through Mark's confused mind streaked the realization that he had to make a stand. He lurched toward Duel, nearly lost his balance. He righted himself, waiting an instant to get his breath.

Duel laughed. "You're in no shape to take a bride."

The towering Charlie Santo grinned. "Shame to waste a young filly like her on an old hoss like him."

Duel turned his head slightly. "Get the girl. We'll take her with us."

"Put a hand on her!" Mark roared. "And I'll cut you to inch size pieces."

He leaped for his brother, hands outstretched, trying to clutch the throat of the insolent younger man. But Duel, laughing again, moved deftly out of reach. Again Mark tried to reach his brother. Duel sidestepped. On and on came Mark and Duel's laughter grew as the older man swung his mighty fists at empty air. And always there was Duel's mocking laughter. A grayness touched Mark's lips. Goaded by this slippery shadow, Mark tried desperately to end it. The pain grabbed at him now, cruelly. As he made one final lunge to trap Duel in a corner of the room he felt something tear in him. And all of a sudden he felt warm and wet as the open wound spilled through the front of his shirt. The room tilted and he fell. He clawed at the floor to keep from sliding off to the black end of the world.

He had one glimpse of his wife. Behind her was the red-bearded Eddie Toll, holding an arm clamped against the waist of her tight-fitting green dress.

It was the last thing he saw, but he did hear another spate of laughter from Duel as the whole room began to spin. Mark sank down into the warm red death that poured unchecked through his body.

CHAPTER TWENTY-EIGHT

Yale was halfway across the yard when he heard the first shot. He stiffened, wheeling toward the main house. He could see that a man lay in the open doorway, face down. A woman was screaming. At first he thought it was Lucy, then decided it was an older woman. In that moment he had to decide his best move. He'd have only one, of that he was sure. If he guessed wrong it would be all over for him. All over for Lucy.

There was shouting from the house. He heard Duel's name mentioned. He heard Mark, sounding like a tired, sick old man. Gripping one of his revolvers, Yale reached the rear door. The voices were louder now. The door stood ajar. Hampered by the weight and bulge of the extra revolver at his belt, he rushed into the house. He banged his way through a kitchen, smelling stale coffee and food.

At the end of a long hallway he saw figures moving. Because of shadows he was unable to identify them. Quickly he moved past an open doorway. Glancing in he saw a fat woman collapsed on the floor. Probably fainted dead away, for there was no mark on her that he could see. Martha Hatcher.

Now as he neared the front of the house he could see Lucy's pale head over Eddie Toll's shoulder. He knew it was Toll because the man was turned a little to one side, lamplight touching the red spike of his beard. Toll had caught her from behind. Frantically she struggled but he was too strong for her. A few steps in front of them the giant Charlie Santo was peering into the parlor.

And then, as Yale crept nearer, he saw Duel in the parlor, staring contemptuously down at the body of his brother. Mark was dead. There was no doubt of it. A bubbling froth at his lips spread across an Indian rug.

Never in the war, never in his whole life was he stepping on such a hair trigger trap. If only he had the good solid assurance of artillery now to command. Parrott Rifles, muzzles pointed directly at the enemy. To annihilate him in one blast. But he had only himself and two revolvers that did not even belong to him.

Duel was saying, "We'll bring her along with us. Because I don't know how many gunhands my brother's been able to hire. We'll put some miles between us and Rafter A till we get things straightened around—"

Yale came quietly along the corridor. Until he was six feet from Eddie Toll. And a board creaked. The sound so loud that Toll flinched and turned his head.

Desperately Yale tried to duplicate his feat at Madam Telfer's when he had smashed Charlie Santo in the face with a gun barrel. But there was too much distance for Yale to cover. Toll twisted aside, taking the full power of the descending gun barrel on his shoulder. There was the *chonking* sound of bone giving way under steel. Toll screamed from the pain of the fractured shoulder. He fell to one knee. With his good hand he was trying to reach his gun. Santo's big body was whipping around. Deeper in the parlor Duel Ashfork jerked up from the body of his brother.

Lucy's cry of fear was smothered as Yale spun her roughly out of Toll's reach, and sent her headlong down the corridor behind him. Until this moment he had not dared fire because of the danger that she might be hit. And she was still exposed, lying flat in the hallway. But he knew full well what life she'd have after these three were through with her. So she had to suffer the risks. There just was no other way.

A thunder of hoofbeats rode the night wind from the east, and he thought of the five men who had ridden the Rafter A road earlier. Probably learned from Burkhalter and the other man that Yale Braden was riding hell bent for Rafter A.

Duel had also heard them. He stood with head cocked.

Everything happened so swiftly it was only a heartbeat ago that Toll's shoulder was crushed. Crouched now, he managed to free his gun. Yale never did remember drawing his second revolver. But it was in his left hand. He fired it into Toll's face, in the thickest part of the beard. Toll slid down the wall, his eyes dead.

Charlie Santo had twisted squarely around, his frame nearly blocking the hall. And in that instant Yale knew he could never make it. And as Santo fired he prayed that Lucy, lying on the floor behind him would not be hit. Nothing else mattered but that.

141

Duel was yelling at Santo, as the big man's first bullet tore into the wall beside Yale's head.

"Don't hit the girl!" Duel cried. "She's Mark's widow—we need her."

If Santo heard Duel at all there was no reaction. The eyes in the face that had been scarred by Yale's gun barrel the day DeLong was killed, were intent on their target.

Again it was the left hand gun, the one Yale had taken from the Rafter A rider on the ranch road, that crashed. He saw Santo flinch. Although Yale had never considered himself ambidexterous, he found a proficiency in snapping back the hammers of the weapons with either thumb.

Even before he saw the orange-red spurt of flame from Santo's gun, he felt the shock in his left arm. The force so great he was half-turned, off balance. The left hand gun might as well have been greased cat. It went sliding out of his fingers. But he retained his grip on the other weapon.

He heard Santo laugh. Yale fired. Santo's laughter ended in a choking sob, a curse. Duel was yelling for Santo to stand aside, to expose Yale Braden. Santo's knees buckled. The big body slowly caved until the final great crashing against the floor. And with Santo no longer blocking the hall, there was Duel, gun up, ready. Yale reeled from one wall to the other with Duel's shot so close it twitched the hair.

Yale dropped to one knee, left arm dangling. As he went down he fired twice. Trying to count his shots. Trying to remember. Another blast from Duel's gun. A bracket lamp was shattered. The hall went dark.

"Step out, blue-belly!" Duel taunted. "Step out where a man can see you!"

Yale didn't step out, he flung himself out. As if catapulted from the hall. At knee height. Straight into the parlor. Duel's aim was too high. The shot blasted across the top of Yale's head. Yale flung himself to one side. Something raked the side of his neck. He felt a lash of blood against his flesh. In the yard men were shouting.

Yale struck the floor with such a crash it jarred his breath. He rolled, came up. His gun was a cannon. Sergeant, elevate thirty-five degrees. The enemy not a mile away, but five feet away. The artillery piece flung the charge upward with such force that the target was smashed.

Well done, Sergeant.

The target had eyes. There was blank astonishment on a handsome dark face.

The lips said, "Why, why? You beat us in the war. You beat us outa Sedalia. You beat us here. You act tall as a mountain, Yankee man——"

Yale's vision cleared. The smashed target was Duel Ashfork. Sitting on the floor, a stain the size of a giant oak leaf growing across his chest. Duel with enough strength to lift a gun. Yale moved his own gun on the floor, tilting the barrel. The hammer snapped, making a sound like the butt end of a hatchet on a dry stick.

Empty.

Duel laughed.

From the doorway a bullet was driven into the crown of Duel's hat. Into the back of his head. The target was down for good. Dead down.

Yale saw the doorway spread wide, narrow. Men poured through. Bill Striker had three faces. He came up, holding three guns that smoked. He peered down at Duel.

"I finally got the son-of-a-bitch, Yale."

Lucy proved to be as adept at nursing as Thela Wheatley. It took some patching to stop the bleeding at his neck.

In the parlor milled Yale's crew and Eph Peters and the hill crowd who had come to fight. Striker had left the Half Pine way station to persuade Peters to lend a hand in the inevitable showdown.

. . . . .

It was decreed that Rafter A would be operated jointly by Lucy, her relatives and the Peters clan. Because all of them had suffered so greatly at the hands of the Ashforks.

Yale Braden built a new house at 88 for his bride. And as the winds changed course Ardin Southworth decided that those running Rafter A and 88 were persons of power.

"Yes, sir." Southworth said to a drummer in the Rincon Hardware, six months after the Rafter A war, "that Yale Braden is mighty fine. And his wife Lucy used to live in that big 'dobe at the top of the hill. The Camacho woman lives there now."

"What happened to the Wheatleys?"

"After they took his badge, Josh got a job as wagon boss for the H and R outfit near Santa Fe. Thela run off with a cattle buyer from Abilene."

"You don't say. Folks miss the Ashforks around here?"

"Not one bit. I was against them from the first," Ardin Southworth stated firmly. "Yale Braden was always my man. A Yankee, maybe, but the best thing that ever happened to Rincon. Yes, sir. Best thing that ever happened."

"Reckon they must spend a lot of money in town these days."

"A whole lot of money. A real lot of money."

Ardin Southworth beamed, rubbed his hands together and glanced in the direction of the ledger that held the accounts for 88, Rafter A and the old Hatcher place south of Rincon.

Dudley Dean was the name Dudley Dean McGaughey used from the beginning of his series of exemplary Western novels written for Fawcett Gold Medal in the 1950s. McGaughey was born in Rialto, California, and began writing fiction for Street & Smith's *Wild West Weekly* in the early 1930s under the name Dean Owen. These early stories, and many more longer pulp novels written for *Masked Rider Western* and *Texas Rangers* after the Second World War, were aimed at a youthful readership. The 1950s marked McGaughey's Golden Age and virtually all that he wrote as Dudley Dean, Dean Owen, or Lincoln Drew during this decade repays a reader with rich dividends in tense storytelling and historical realism. This new direction can be seen in short novels he wrote early in the decade such as 'Gun the Man Down' in *5 Western Novels* (8/52) and 'Hang the Man High!' in *Big-Book Western* (3/54). They are notable for their maturity and presage the dramatic change in tone and characterization that occurs in the first of the Dudley Dean novels, *Ambush at Rincon* (1953). *The Man from Riondo* (1954), if anything, was even better, with considerable scope in terms of locations, variety of characters and unusual events. *Gun in the Valley* (1957) by Dudley Dean, *Chainlink* (1957) by Owen Evens, and *Rifle Ranch* (1958) by Lincoln Drew are quite probably his finest work among the fine novels from this decade. These stories are notable in particular for the complexity of their social themes and psychological relationships, but are narrated in a simple, straightforward style with such deftly orchestrated plots that their subtlety and depth may become apparent only upon reflection.